BARRACUDA

THE FIGHTING ANTHONYS
BOOK THREE

BARRACUDA

by

Michael Aye

BOSON BOOKS
Raleigh

LAND O'LAKES BRANCH

Michael Aye is a retired Naval Medical Officer. He has long been a student of early American and British Naval history. Since reading his first Kent novel, Mike has spent many hours reading the great authors of sea fiction, often while being "haze gray and underway" himself.

http://michaelaye.com

© 2009 Michael A. Fowler

Published by
Boson Books, a division of C & M Online Media, Inc.
3905 Meadow Field Lane,
Raleigh, NC 27606-4470
cm@cmonline.com

http://www.bosonbooks.com
http://www.bosonromances.com

ISBN (paper): 1-932482-61-X
ISBN (ebook): 1-932482-62-8

Cover art by Carrie Skalla
Designed by Megan Roberts

This is a work of fiction and is not an account of actual historical events.

Dedication

This book is dedicated to Ray Knight and Nancy Lopez for their friendship, generosity and endless support to my grandson, my family and me during a period of personal tragedy. Truly these are two of God's special angels and our family will never forget their efforts.

Table of Contents

viii

Acknowledgments

I would like to issue a special "Bravo Zulu" to Dave and Nancy at Boson Books. Without these wonderful people *HMS SeaWolf* would have been sunk before the keel ever cut deep water. Due to their continued support *Barracuda* now sets sail.

I would like to thank that one special lady who doesn't want her name mentioned but without her help there wouldn't have been a manuscript. She edits; critiques and doesn't let me get by with mediocrity.

Special thanks to Carrie Skalla for her art work. She is truly a talented young lady who has spent many hours creating the artwork for the Fighting Anthonys series.

Also a special thanks to the Skalla family for always being there in a time of need and their willingness to lend a helping hand.

I want to thank you, "the reader" for not only buying *The Reaper* and *HMS SeaWolf*, but demanding Book Three, *Barracuda*. I hope you enjoy this and future installments of the Fighting Anthonys series.

PART I

Battle Fatigue

I take a breath and look around me.
I'm grateful to be alive.
The guns, they're all silent now,
But, the smoke still burns my eyes.
There's a heaviness within me,
It takes a heavy toll.
It burns like rum going down,
To an empty, aching soul.

-Michael Aye

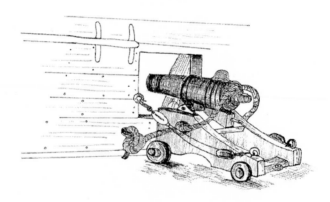

Prologue

WHIRRR...BOOM!

WHIRRR...BOOM!

"Damme, Mr. Decker, what's that?"

"We're being attacked, sir," a trembling wild-eyed midshipman answered the fourth lieutenant of HMS Diamond 64.

WHIRRR...BOOM!

CRASH!..."Watch out, zur, the foremast 'as been hit," a scrambling seaman shouted out as he ran by, looking back at the wild-eyed midshipman.

Brown, the fourth lieutenant snarled, "Aye, we're being attacked, Mr. Decker, but by whom and how in God's name did they get this close without being sighted?"

BOOM!...BOOM!...

Dozen's of shadowy figures came up from below decks. Among the half-crazed men, Mr. Knight, the ship's first lieutenant, was still dressing as he made his way on deck.

BOOM!...KABOOM!...

Flames came spurting up like a bonfire from a nearby vessel.

"That's the mail packet, sir, the HMS Mosquito."

"Well, I hope to hell all the mails off," Knight answered sarcastically, then stared at Brown. "Beat to quarters, Mr. Brown."

"Aye, sir. Bosun!"

"Aye, Mr. Brown."

"Beat to quarters."

"Aye, aye, sir."

BOOM!...BOOM!...

The assault continued... then another explosion.

"Damned if we aren't being attacked by a fleet, Mr. Brown. I believe a cannon fires about every time I take a breath," Lieutenant Knight exclaimed.

Then as if to emphasize his remarks the whole ship seem to shudder as another ball had found its target.

"Where's Captain Stafford?" Knight asked.

"He...ah...sent a note aboard with his cox'n, sir, and said he'd be ashore tonight, but I'm sure he's heard the cannons so he's bound to be on his way back," the frightened Decker stammered.

"No doubt our captain is awake," Knight responded, "But what about those fools in the fort? They've not fired a shot."

"Mr. Knight!" It was Williams, the carpenter, "We're sinking sir. We've got over three feet in the well and it's gaining." Then as an after thought he continued, "The pumps have either been destroyed or what's left can't keep up."

"Well, hell's fire, we've been attacked by God knows who, the fort is yet to fire a shot and Commodore Meriwether's flagship is going to sink right here at the entrance of Saint Augustine Harbour."

BOOM!...CRASH!...

Another ball had scored a hit and overturned a cannon. Wounded men were crying out in agony while others were cursing. Then another explosion as the schooner, HMS Amsterdam, was hit and immediately engulfed in flames.

"Does anyone know where the Commodore is?" Knight asked the group in front of him, a group that had increased in numbers, as the men came forward looking for direction.

"Ah...," this again from the midshipman Decker, "Sir Percival is being entertained ashore this evening as well, sir."

"Well, it better be a hellish fine entertainment to make up for what's in store when he faces the Admiral."

"Sir!" a pleading Williams cried. "What about all these men?" gesturing to the wounded that lay about.

Knight could see four sets of sails rounding the bend from the south. Had they even gotten off a shot, he wondered. Was this to end his career? Surely there would be a court martial and he'd been in the Navy long enough to know "shat ran downhill".

Diamond shook as she was hit again with splashes all around indicating several near misses.

"Mr. Brown!"

"*Aye, sir!*"

"*Prepare to abandon ship. Make sure the wounded are carried off first and send for the gunner and any of his mates still left alive. I want every gun still usable made ready to fire.*"

Bewildered Brown asked, "*To what purpose, sir?*"

"*Honour!*" *Knight roared back.* "*Damn your soul. Honour! Now get moving!*"

"*Aye, sir!*"

Chapter One

This way Lord Anthony, Admiral Howe will see you now."

Anthony thanked the flag lieutenant as he was ushered into the admiral's stateroom. After thanking the lieutenant, Anthony turned and was face to face with Vice Admiral Richard (Black Dick) Howe, commander of His Majesty's Naval Forces in North America.

Anthony knew the meeting would be short. It was getting late and the temperature was dropping. There had already been snow flurries across New York's harbour.

"Well, Gil, it's a fine show you put on for those damnable privateers trying to take Nova Scotia. Had they succeeded, the war would have been over before it started. You're to be commended, sir. I read your report and you've a fine bunch of officers. I like it when a commander recognizes his men for their efforts. Now, have a glass of hot brandy, sir. It will warm you as there's precious little heat on board this ship."

As the two sat down a silence filled the admiral's quarters until the brandy was poured.

"Would you care for a stick of cinnamon in your drink, Gil? It's something the Colonials do."

"No, my Lord, I take it plain."

"Fine, now shoo…shoo…Walters, go find a warm spot." It was the admiral's way of sending off the servant.

"Hard to find a good servant that doesn't talk," Howe said as the servant departed.

When the door was closed Howe started again, "Have you heard about that business in Saint Augustine?"

"Only bits and pieces, my Lord."

"Well it was a shame. A damned utter shame, I tell you. Four ships lost, one the commodore's own flagship, while he and the ship's captain were being entertained for the evening. Entertained, huh! Dipping their wicks I'd wager. Sir Percival is near sixty. I can just see that flabby fat arse of his being entertained. Cost him; cost him a guinea or more I'd wager. Well, I've sent him home. Hopefully we'll not hear from him again but his kind always seems to pop up, usually in Parliament. I'm giving you his job, not that he did anything with it, but I've different expectations of you. I've read your record, Gil. You're destined, sir, and damme if I don't envy you. 'Course Lord James was destined too," Lord Howe said speaking of Anthony's father. "That being said you mind yourself."

Anthony took a deep breath but said nothing, allowing Admiral Howe to continue.

"Now let's get down to business. Privateers are costing us this war. I know it and you know it, I just wished Lord North would realize it. The south is a haven for the rouges. We control the east coast of Florida as you know but some think she's ripe for the picking."

"Privateers roam with impunity from the Carolina's down along the coast of Florida, through the keys to Cuba, even into the Gulf of Mexico. Florida's governor, Patrick Tonyn, has requested help. He says he'll have it; else the damn Spaniards and Rebels will have Florida before we know it. He's a steady man so I believe him.

Hell, just this fall the damn privateers took the brig, *HMS Betsy*, within site of Saint Augustine. She was full of gunpowder when she was taken and not a damnable thing could Tonyn do but watch. In his letter for help he states he's only got four hundred muskets to defend the entire border of Florida. Not much of a force would you say?"

But before Anthony could reply, Howe continued without hardly pausing.

"You are going to change that. Not only are you going to make a presence, your going to make it felt."

"Aye," Anthony acknowledged. It was somewhat humorous how Lord Howe had gotten his temper up talking about the privateers and Lord North. *Which stirred him the most?* Anthony wondered. Lord Howe had risen from his chair and paced the deck as he ranted. He now sat down behind his desk and took out a document.

Handing it to Anthony, he continued, "You're going to lose Moffett."

Surprised Anthony stared directly at Lord Howe. A smile crept across Howe's face. "Moffett has made admiral. He will sail back with Pope on *HMS Drakkar* to England for his orders." Raising his hand to fend off Lord Anthony's objections Howe continued, "I know you don't want to lose *Drakkar* but she's been out here for over three years and it's time she returns for an overhaul. I thought Moffett would like to hear about his promotion from you."

"Thank you, my Lord." Anthony regained his composure and asked, "Is there a replacement named?"

"Aye, I thought you might want Captain Buck."

A frown creased Anthony's brow.

"You don't want him?" Howe questioned.

"Oh no, my Lord, I mean yes, my Lord, I do, but who'll command *HMS Merlin*?"

"I thought you might have someone in mind," Lord Howe responded.

"I do sir, but I've just given him command...ere... temporary command of a captured French corvette."

"Yes, I read that in your report. Is she seaworthy?"

"Aye, my Lord, she's had repairs and is ready."

"Fine then," Howe answered. "I'll make Earl captain on *Merlin* and I'm going to promote Knight and give him command of your captured corvette."

"Knight, sir?"

"Yes. He was the first lieutenant on *Diamond*. Were it not for him we'd not fired a shot during the attack at Saint Augustine. He and a volunteer gun crew fired on the hellish privateers until they no longer had a gun left to fire. The decks were awash as the ship was sinking. Had it not been for a gun captain lashing him to a grate he would have gone down with the ship. As it is now he's mending from burns to his arms and chest. I'll not let his bravery go unrewarded. Not by a damn site."

Anthony took a deep breath then asked, "Would it be possible sir...for him to be part of my squadron? I could use a man who has experience in the area."

"Yes, I see your point, though knowing Sir Percival as I do I'm not sure how much local experience he's obtained outside of Saint Augustine's Harbour. However, it would do him good to be attached to a good commander. Very well, he and the ship are yours."

As Anthony made his way back to his barge he felt a pang of jealousy. Damn Pope, lucky sod that he was, returning to England while Anthony had to stay in the Colonies. Anthony thought of his last letter from Deborah. "Heavy with your child" was how she put it. The last time he saw her she didn't even know she was pregnant. However, if she hadn't been it would not have been from a lack of trying. She had never had a child and being pregnant at age thirty was considered risky by Anthony's family physician. Deborah's last letter had assured him her pregnancy was going well. *Slow as the mail is she will have had the baby and it'll be weaned from the tit before I know anything,* Anthony thought.

Seeing the smile on Lord Anthony's face Bart, the admiral's cox'n, volunteered, "Peers 'is Lordship 'as pleased yew. We going home?"

"No, but to a warmer climate," Anthony answered.

"Well, hits bout time, way yews timbers be cracking when yews walking about causes me to shiver."

"My timbers!" Anthony exclaimed. "How could you hear me when you crack and pop worse than a sprung mast in a heavy gale. My timbers...humph."

"Well, I'm guessing the warm airs could do us-uns both a bit o' good," Bart said as he turned to climb down into the admiral's barge leaving Anthony nothing but open sky and water to reply to.

Chapter Two

By noon the wind was near a half gale, lusty but not as bitter as it had been the month before. Still it came fierce and bellowing out of the northeast creating snarling gray waves, rising higher and higher, beating at *HMS SeaWolf's* hull before rushing on to attack the nearby Halifax shoreline.

Lieutenant "Gabe" Anthony, captain of *SeaWolf* stood at the lee rail taking it all in as the ship was being made ready for sea. Since the recent battle with privateers off Nova Scotia, the ship had been newly rigged and painted. Fresh water had been lightered out along with casks of beef, pork and wine as well as countless other supplies.

The new first lieutenant seemed to be everywhere at once. He was old for his age and wizened as he had risen from the lower deck. It was said Admiral "Black Dick" Howe had promoted him on the spot for extraordinary bravery in battle. Lieutenant Jem Jackson may never make admiral, but he was an outstanding first lieutenant.

Thinking of this made Gabe wonder how his last first lieutenant was doing. Everette Hazard had also risen from the ranks. After he had been seriously wounded in the recent battle with privateers, Lord Anthony had taken him on as flag lieutenant.

A loud resonant voice attracted Gabe's attention— Andrew "Andy" Gunnells. The new master was a smallish, premature gray-haired man. His face was leathery and tanned by the sun and wind from countless voyages. He gave an immediate impression of great competence. He had small twinkling eyes and the crow's feet that appeared with his quick grin gave an equal impression of a ready sense of humor. Gabe thought he would probably keep the wardroom on its toes.

Dawkins, Gabe's newly appointed secretary, a man who had been with him from the time he was a midshipman, was approaching. He was bent forward with a scarf over his head trying to keep the wind out of his aching ear. He was sniffling and snorting in spite of the mixture of honey, lemon and brandy Lum had concocted.

Lum was a former slave on a plantation in South Carolina. He had killed the plantation overseer to prevent Faith from being raped. She had begged Gabe to take Lum with him, "else he'll be hanged" she pleaded. So here he was. A giant of a man, loose limbed, almost ungainly, a baldpate with salt and pepper colored hair on the sides. He was solid as a ship's timber with big calloused hands. He was like a demon in battle but like magic could turn to something almost delicate as he played a soulful melody on his lotz.

As Dawkins got close he sounded very nasal as he tried to speak above the wind. "You going to wait on Dagan and Caleb to return before your ready to eat or do you want Lum to fix you something now?"

Realizing that he was indeed hungry and just as important realizing he was creating more of a hindrance by being on deck, Gabe decided to go below then thought to ask, "Did Caleb take his damn ape with him?"

"Aye," Dawkins replied. "There's naught on board to look after the bugger since Lum 'as sworn off him."

Caleb's ape, Mr. Jewells, had tried to pick the gray hairs out of Lum's scalp one night after he had fallen asleep in one of the cabin's chairs. It was dark in the cabin but the pulling sensation caused Lum to wake up and immediately felt a heavy weight upon his lap. The ape was face to face with him so that when he opened his eyes all he could see was the ape's teeth as it rolled its lips. He could feel the hot breath on his face, with two tiny beady eyes staring at him.

Lum let out a scream that startled the ape causing it to let out a blood-curdling scream, which was made worse when Lum's chair fell back hitting the deck and jarring the two apart. The sentry hearing the screams rushed into the cabin only to be run over by the ape trying to escape.

As the two collided, the sentry's musket was knocked from his grip causing it to go off as it hit the deck. The loud shot rang out adding to the confusion. The officer on watch alerted the master-at-arms and sentries were put around the ship fearing attack. By the time Lum, who had been either knocked unconscious falling with the chair or fainted from his fright was able to speak, everything had quieted down.

When asked if the ape had scared him Lum replied, "How'd you like to wake up wid sumthin' plucking at yo' head? Then when you opens yo' eyes all you sees is dem big ole teevies shining at you in da moonlight, and feels dat hot breath blowing on yo's face. Yas suh! I was scared and I ain't shame to say it. No suh! I didn't know if it was a ghost or a sea devil or what, but I knowed it didn't belong in old Lum's lap. No suh, not in a hundred years it didn't."

It was a sleepy-eyed Gabe who made his way on deck. Dagan, as always was at his side. He watched every morning as Gabe dressed and wondered if he'd ever be a good riser. Dagan was not only Gabe's uncle but also his protector, a rite he had assumed upon the death of Gabe's gypsy grandfather.

"Mr. Jackson, Mr. Gunnells." The habitual greeting.

"Morning, captain." The habitual reply.

Damn I'm getting cantankerous, Dagan thought.

"The anchor's hove short, sir, and the men are at their stations prepared to get underway," Jackson volunteered.

"Very well," Gabe replied then turned his attention to the master.

"Winds from the north-nor-east. Not as fresh as she be yesterday but it'll be a brisk one by any man's thinking."

Nodding his understanding to Gunnells, Gabe directed his attention back to his first lieutenant. "Well, Mr. Jackson, you've worked wonders putting *SeaWolf* back to rights. Now sir, you may have the privilege of putting us to sea."

"Aye! Aye! Captain." A smile on Jackson's face as he turned to go about his duties, pleased the captain had so quickly placed his confidence in him.

Pipes shrilled and the deck came alive. New replacement seamen were urged on by curses from the petty officers. Gabe could feel *SeaWolf* tugging on the cable as the wind freshened. The fiddler plucked out an Irish shanty—attempts to please its new master no doubt.

"Now me little sweethearts, let's give the ladies in Halifax a final wave to remember us by." This from the bosun, Graf.

"Hands aloft. Prepare to make sail," Jackson bellowed as seamen scrambled to do his bidding.

"Loosen mainsails! Lively now, lads. You heard the lieutenant," Graf shouted.

The sails suddenly filled with the wind giving a thunderous flap.

From forward, Nathan Lavery, the second lieutenant cried out, "Anchors aweigh."

Gabe could hear the clank, clank, clank as the capstan continued to reel in the anchor. Looking over at the compass, the helmsman volunteered, "South by sou'east, sir."

Glancing forward Gabe could see the men had the anchor hauled towards the cathead. Jackson was ordering Lavery to have the yards braced around to take full advantage of the wind. The headland and most of the shoreline seemed to be disappearing very quickly as the wind held steady. *SeaWolf* plunged through the cresting waves cascading spray over the bow.

Approaching Gabe, Jackson stated, "I'd like to see how she behaves under full canvas if you don't mind, sir."

"Very well, Mr. Jackson, put her through her courses, and then get some food in the men." Looking at Dagan and giving a slight motion with his head Gabe turned back to Jackson, "I'm going to my cabin. I'm sure you have control of the ship and can do without my presence for a time." Then, before Jackson could respond, Gabe headed down the ladder to his cabin.

"Seems to be ready to head south, don't he?" Dagan said as he closed the cabin door.

"Aye, and so am I," Gabe said. "I wish we had been able to sail with Gil and the squadron when they left. I've had enough of this cold. I'm ready for some warm weather."

Dagan watched as Gabe unconsciously clutched the empty pouch around his neck. Aye, Dagan thought, warm weather and closer to the pretty little rebel girl who held his heart and his ruby. Feeling the stiffness between his shoulder, Dagan thought maybe a little warm weather would do some good. Either that or drink some of Caleb's willow bark tea he prescribes for the agues.

Chapter Three

It was to be a grand affair, the likes of which neither Bart, Silas or any other of Lord Anthony's staff could ever remember.

"It's time for a feast," Lord Anthony had shouted out to Silas as he entered his stateroom. Then while reading the letters that had been laid on his desk he gave a whoop and declared, "Well, damme." Bart had entered the cabin at that time and knew something was in the wind. He'd never seen his Lordship take on so.

Seeing his cox'n, Anthony ordered, "See the flag captain, Bart, and have him signal for all captains to repair on board with their first lieutenants to dine with the admiral this evening. Soon as that's done hurry on back and we'll share a wet."

Hum, thought Bart, *something was definitely up*. More 'n one something likely and he bet he knew what half of it had to be, seeing as he put the thick letter from Lady Deborah on the admiral's desk. A smile crept across Bart's face. With his lordship carrying on so he'd forgotten to mention *SeaWolf* was just entering the harbour. Now Gabe would be on hand to enjoy the celebration. Bart quickened his pace; maybe he could put a word in the flag captain's ear to keep quiet about *SeaWolf* for a spell.

With the help of Moffett's chef and servant, Silas
had put on a feast to remember. It was a harassed flag
lieutenant who had gotten back aboard just in time with
a rump of beef that was to be the centerpiece of the
table. Last minute shopping was not his idea of a flag
lieutenant's duties but he was willing to do his best for his
admiral on such a grand occasion. The rump had been
boiled and the brisket had been roasted. The tongue and
tripe was minced and baked into pies. A young kid goat
was dressed in its own blood and thyme with a pudding
in its belly. After that came a shoulder of mutton with a
side of goat both covered with a rasher of bacon. As
though that wasn't enough for all the captains and their
first lieutenants to gorge themselves senseless, there was
pickled oysters, bowls of potatoes and vegetables. Finally,
Silas served a dish of his famous berry pastries and apple
tarts.

With the desserts finished, glasses of sherry were
poured as clay pipes and cigars were passed. Once the
pipes were billowing and cigars were lighted, Lord
Anthony stood and raised his glass for a toast. As he
stood he glanced Gabe's way. Gabe, seeing Lord
Anthony's gaze, smiled and nodded ever so slightly. He
had been made privy to her ladyship's news and had
already congratulated his brother.

"Gentlemen, it is my pleasure to inform each of you
that my wife, Lady Deborah, has presented your admiral
with a child, a baby girl. She has been named Macayla
Rose.

A cry went up, "Here, here, to Lady Deborah and
Lord Anthony." As the officers settled down Anthony
had the glasses recharged and again stood.

"Gentlemen, it is now my pleasure to present to you
the Royal Navies newest admiral. Admiral Dutch
Moffett."

Again the cheers from the officers. When it had quieted down Anthony stood again.

"A toast to the new flag captain. Captain Buck."

Another round of cheers that took a time to settle down. When Anthony had everyone's attention, "A toast to Captain Stephen Earl, *HMS Merlin*."

This time the cheers took longer as Earl was not only made captain but was given *Merlin*. After the group had finished congratulating Earl, Lord Anthony stood again.

"Gentlemen, this night should prove a night like no other. We are here to say farewell to Captain Pope who is returning to England with *Drakkar* for a much needed refitting." This time instead of cheers, good-natured boos. Once the noise quieted down, Anthony continued, "He will have the honor of carrying with him our new admiral, Admiral Moffett. However, as one shipmate departs we welcome a new one. Gentlemen, I present Master and Commander, Sir Raymond Knight, Captain of the Navy's latest prize, *HMS LeFrelon*."

Once more the cheers and toast. Meanwhile, Bart and Dagan had ambled aft, and were leaning on the taffrail having a wet, smoking their pipes, and having a quiet conversation. The aroma of burnt tobacco filled the air causing Johns, the fifth lieutenant who had the watch to look aft. Seeing the old seadogs he was touched. It was men like these that took care of men like those below in the admiral's quarters that really made the Navy what it was.

Another cheer from below. Hearing it, Johns felt a pang of jealously and wished he could join the party. Not the one below, but the one at the taffrail.

Chapter Four

The gale force Atlantic winds carried the two ships along under full sail. *SeaWolf* and *HMS Swan* had been given orders to carry dispatches to Admiral Graves, whose squadron was thought to be somewhere between the West Indies, meaning Antigua, and Philadelphia.

Upon delivering the dispatches, *SeaWolf* and *Swan*, were to join Admiral Lord Anthony at Saint Augustine. They had been ordered to sail together because of the increasing menace of privateers.

Lieutenant Markham, who commanded *Swan*, and Gabe had both received the benefit of serving as midshipman under Lord Anthony. Therefore, most of the time, they were of the same mindset. This was in evidence at the rate of speed, a full seven knots in a wind when most would have taken in a sail.

SeaWolf's First Lieutenant Jackson was in deep conversation with Nathan Lavery, the second lieutenant, and the only other officer aboard the ship. Dagan observed the two as he stood by the lee rail. Undoubtedly, Jackson was pleased at what Lavery was telling him as a smile creased the otherwise hard leathery face. Were they talking about some adventure ashore, about their captain or some doxy? Which ever made no difference? They were happy and generally happy officers meant a happy crew.

Andy Gunnells, the ship's master, was aft trying to light his pipe, too stubborn to duck below the rail out of the wind—an Irishman, whose favorite phrase seems to be "God Save Ireland." A plume of smoke, the pipe had finally been lit and Gunnells ambled towards Dagan.

As he made his way he paused and cocked his head so that his right ear was pointed south. Dagan knew what caused Gunnells to cock his ear. He had just heard it too. Gunfire. No sooner had the thought come to mind than several seamen stopped what they were doing and faced forward.

"Lookout! Damme man, I'm calling you," Jackson bellowed. "Do you have anything to report?"

"No, sir," the lookout called down, "Clear to larboard and starboard. A bit 'o 'aze be blocking the view forward, sir."

Hearing either the gunfire or the lookout's report brought Gabe on deck. Dagan wasn't sure but had expected Jackson to send a messenger for him. Gabe was about to order another lookout be sent aloft when to his surprise Jackson headed up the futtock shrouds with his glass. Then, like a true sailor, shunned the lubbers hole as he found a place to perch, nudging the lookout over a bit.

There was a bit of haze, as the lookout had stated, but to a trained eye powder smoke was also visible. Looking at the sailor seated next to him with a degree of disgust, Jackson called down his sighting.

Hearing the report, Gabe called Midshipman Lancaster, "Make a signal to *Swan*. Gunfire."

"Is that all, sir?" Lancaster asked.

"Aye, lad, Captain Markham needs no further information at present."

Swan had been to windward and about half a league behind *SeaWolf*. At sighting the signal, Markham had her brought up to within hailing distance.

"Sail ho!" The shout came from the masthead. Jackson who had returned to the deck looked up waiting for the report to continue.

"Off the starboard bow, a brig by 'er tops'ls. Hull and mains'ls still down yit."

Gabe couldn't control his agitation. "Any other ships, anything in chase?"

"No, sir." Then after a pause, "Another ship 'as come outta the 'aze sir. A big un, a frigate she be. Her sails be red and yellow, sir."

"Whose sails man?" Jackson shouted out. "The brig or the frigate?"

"The frigate, sir. No flag but 'er sails look like a Dago's. She be luffin," cried the lookout.

This time there was no doubt when the distant ship fired. The heavy explosion filled the air. Gabe watched through his glass as a thundercloud of acrid smoke billowed out from the larger ship, reeking havoc on the small brig. Another racking explosion.

Damme thought Gabe. *That cutthroat's gunners know their business.*

"Mr. Druett!"

"Aye, captain."

"Double charge the bowchaser but no ball. See if we can attract the whoreson's attention."

"Aye, cap'n," Druett answered, then was off.

A confused Midshipman Lancaster looked to Dagan, "No ball?" he asked.

"Aye, lad. With a double charge it will sound like we have a heavy gun and if they can't see the splash of ball they won't know how close we are."

An old trick Gabe's father had discussed during one of his many talks. *So the boy had been paying attention,* Dagan thought. If the old admiral could see his son now he'd be proud.

Again a terrific blast from the Spaniard ship, enveloping both ships in smoke. As the smoke cleared the Spanish vessel appeared to be hauling her wind. Maybe she had spied *Swan* and *SeaWolf*. Although together the pair would present little or no challenge for the frigate.

Training his glass back on the hapless brig Gabe realized here was the reason for the frigate's departure. The brig was listing badly to larboard, most of the upper structure gone. Mast riggings, bulwark, transom all shot away. The poor ship was sinking. The frigate had completed its deadly task. No boats were in the water, so undoubtedly they were destroyed as well. A few of the crew could be seen on deck. A grating was lowered over the side, apparently with wounded strapped to it. Gabe turning to Dagan said, "I wonder how much help Caleb will be."

Out of the brigs full complement only twenty-seven survived the vicious pounding by the frigate. The senior survivor was the carpenter, a man oddly enough named Woods, John Woods.

"We were carrying uniforms, boots and such," he explained. "Few cases of muskets with powder and shot to go along, but no great cargo; so we were sailing without escort. Then along comes this ship flying his Spanish colors. Since we weren't at war with Spain the captain didn't seem to be too concerned. She can overtake us at any turn, he told me shipmate, Bundy. Then the frigate hauls down her colors but stead of boarding us like the cap'n figures she'll do, she just opens her gun ports and blasts away."

"Maybe she saw us," Jackson volunteered.

"Begging your pardon sir," Woods answered the first lieutenant. "I don't think she was to much worried about a brigantine and a schooner. Bundy, he's...he was the ship's master, said it was almost like the *Barracuda* had a score to settle with us."

"The *Barracuda*?"

"Aye, sir, that was the name on the frigate. The *Barracuda*."

Later, when things had settled down Gabe, Caleb and Dagan sat in Gabe's cabin. Each man nursing a glass of wine and listened as Lum played a tune on his lotz. The sun had all but set, but what was left sent a prism of colors across the stern as it was reflected from the cold ocean waters. Trying to see out the windows was now difficult as they were caked with salt. *SeaWolf* along with *Swan* drove further and further to the southwest.

Gabe waited till Lum had finished his melody then spoke, "Do you know what today's incident reminds me of?"

"I was thinking along those lines as well," Dagan replied. "Makes you think of the *Reaper*."

"Yes, but her captain was French and he's dead," Caleb interjected.

"Aye, he is," Dagan replied, "But Montique's not. That's something we can't afford to forget."

"No," Gabe replied, "I'll not soon forget."

"Nor will I," Dagan promised himself as he took another swig of his wine. "Nor will I."

Chapter Five

Gabe, Gunnells, the master, and the first lieutenant, Jackson, sat reviewing the charts they had of Saint Augustine, Florida. They had been able to rendezvous with Admiral Graves the day following the incident between the brig and the *Barracuda*.

Admiral Graves showed little concern about the incident other than to say he could use the survivors to replace men lost from his ships, men Gabe had hoped would be used to augment Lord Anthony's squadron. But Admiral Graves being an admiral and Gabe being a lieutenant, the men went where Graves dictated.

Now Gunnells was going over different channels into Saint Augustine Harbour. "The North channel is deeper but narrow, while the South channel is much wider. However, there's a sandbar with only eight to nine feet of water at low tide with breakers separating both of the South channels entrances."

"Along here," the master explained using calipers to point with, "The water is also shallow with more breakers. His Lordship's flagship and the frigate will have to anchor just off the north breaker while it's possible for *SeaWolf*, *Swan*, *Pigeon* and *Audacity* to enter the harbour. I'm not sure about *LeFrelon*. More than likely

Audacity will be in much use plying between the anchorage and Saint Augustine."

"Audacity's captain won't much like his new livelihood I'm thinking," Jackson said with a smile on his face.

"It's in the scriptures already I'm betting," Gunnells responded.

"What about the harbour and the city?" Gabe asked the old master.

"Several rivers, the Matanzas, San Sebastions, and St. Marks all flow into the harbour. Most places there's nigh on to thirty feet, so if there was a deep channel there'd be a good anchorage. The harbour sets between Anastasia Island and Saint Augustine. There's a lighthouse on Anastasia Island. There's a huge castle that's been turned into a fort right here in Saint Augustine, but I don't see it being much help. I was here in '70 and the cannons looked ancient then. I'd be afraid to fire one if they haven't been replaced. More 'n likely kill more of us than the enemy," the old master said, matter-of-factly. "They were probably put there by the Spaniards when they first built the place two hunered years ago."

Then, turning back to the charts Gunnells said, "I'm betting the squadron will be at anchorage here," using his pipe as a pointer. "That being said, we should drop anchor alongside the flagship by midday, Lord willing."

Admiral Lord Anthony stepped down from the coach as a footman opened the door. The man continued holding the door as Everette Hazard dressed in his finest as the flag lieutenant, made his way out of the coach. If the footman noticed the pinned sleeve he made no sign. Hazard was somewhat self-conscious of his one empty sleeve and was bewildered at Lord Anthony's offer to make him his flag lieutenant. He could never remember a one-armed flag lieutenant, certainly not one who had just been promoted to lieutenant after serving before the mast. Gabe had something to do with this appointment, he was sure.

While only a lieutenant himself, Gabe was Admiral Lord Anthony's brother, so there was little doubt in Hazard's mind as to where the recommendation had come from. Once he had asked Bart, the admiral's cox'n if he thought he could handle the requirements.

"Sure yew can. Alls yews got to do is stand around making sure 'is lordship is taken care of proper like when theys guest and dignaterry's about. Course yew got to fetch and carry his lordship's 'portant papers and such but yew's a do fine."

"But why would he choose me," Hazard pressed on seeking to confirm his suspicions that Gabe had been instrumental in his appointment.

Bart's reply was solemn and as elementary as Hazard had ever heard. "'Cause us-un's take care of our own." Stated so, Hazard never asked another question. This was his first ceremonial task as the new flag lieutenant and he wanted to do a good job and show the admiral his confidence in him had not been misplaced.

The two other footmen, who seemed to appear just at the precise moment, pulled a pair of heavy ornate doors open. Once inside Government House a clerk greeted the pair and ushered them into the governor's office. Anthony glanced at Everette and smiled to himself. Everette seemed awestruck as he took in the pillared corridor, and the huge paintings that lined the walls.

As the usher approached a large painted door he stepped to the side to let Anthony and Everette pass

through before he announced, "Admiral Lord Anthony
and his flag lieutenant, sir."

Governor Patrick Tonyn stood from behind his desk
to greet his visitors. He was debonair and elegantly
dressed in all white. He had a firm handshake and you
got the feeling he was a man qualified for the job at
hand. "A glass of wine, my Lord, lieutenant?"

As both officers responded, Governor Tonyn sent a
servant for the wine then had the men seat themselves.
When the servant returned Tonyn explained as the two
men looked at their glasses.

"Sangria, gentlemen. One of the Spanish wines that
I find light and refreshing for the midday. Some may
think it sweet after drinking the usual dry British wine."

The wine was sweeter than Anthony was used to,
but it did have a pleasant taste and was chilled.

"Have you ever been to Florida, my Lord?" Tonyn
asked.

"No, I've not had the privilege."

"Then let me fill you in on some of the history which
I think will better able you to carry out your orders. In
1763, Havana was given to the Spanish for the Province
of Florida. Most of the Spanish residents chose to depart
for Cuba. However, some stayed. Mostly the very poor,
many blacks and individuals of mixed blood. Even a few
of the wealthier stayed to maintain their extensive
properties. I'm sure most in this group are actually
spies."

"In November 1775, I issued a proclamation that
invited loyal subjects who were being harassed by the
rebels in the northern colonies to come to Florida and
we would give them land to start anew. Since then rebels
out of Savannah, Georgia and surrounding areas have
raided us. They kill, plunder then make their way back
to safety before I even know they've been a foot."

"I ordered a number of forts built to help defend us from these invasions. I've authorized a force of militia to be raised. A man of considerable merit, Thomas Browne, commands the militia. You will meet him and others at a meeting tomorrow."

"Now one other thing. Admiral Howe is shipping us prisoners of war. Some of which are well to do. If the prisoners give their parole, I give them the freedom of the city. Others are being kept on the sloop, *Otter*, which has been turned into a prison ship and still others are kept at the lighthouse."

Tonyn who had been sitting on his desk while talking let out a deep sigh, then stood up. Glancing at the remaining wine he put the glass to his lips and finished the fruity liquid.

"Now sir, you've heard of the damn privateers taking the *Betsy* and her load of gunpowder right on our doorsteps. Then another group had the audacity to sail right into our harbour and fire on our ships and town. Had it not been for Lieutenant Knight, we'd never have fired a shot in return. Now we seem to be in danger of losing all our supply ships without which we can't survive. A day will come when we are self-sufficient. However, we are not there yet. Your job, admiral, is to make the coast of Florida too hot for these damn rogues."

Sitting in his chair while letting the governor speak had given Anthony's knee time to stiffen up so he stretched out his legs, flexed them, and then stood up.

"Do you have any idea as to the location the privateers might be using as a main base?"

"Anywhere! Hell man! The Keys is full of coves suitable for hiding. There's fresh water on most of them and deep water anchoring at some. Cuba is only a short distance from the Keys. However, the rogues could just as well be anywhere from Savannah to the Carolinas."

Lowering his eyes and shaking his head, Tonyn said in truth, "I have no clue where the base is or if there is a specific base. As I said before, I'm sure some of our esteemed Spanish citizens are nothing more than spies, keeping the rebels well informed."

Then the governor returned to his chair behind the large desk. The meeting was over. As Tonyn shook Anthony's hand he said, "I will do all I can to support you but without the supply ships we can't even support ourselves. I wish you God's speed and good hunting, Admiral."

Chapter Six

Master and Commander Sir Raymond Knight had not gotten use to the new title, or to the command of *HMS LeFrelon*. The ship was a captured French corvette of twenty guns. However, as per Royal Navy protocol the day he had taken command as master and commander she ceased to be a corvette and became a sloop.

He was also amazed at the attitude and relationship between Admiral Anthony and the other captains and officers under his command. They all seemed to be so at ease and unafraid to voice their thoughts and recommendations when asked, unlike Commodore Meriwether's officers, who were afraid to speak due to his endless ridicule and sarcasm.

Standing in the admiral's cabin, Knight was still awed at the spacious, even elegant place. It had to be over thirty feet wide. The mahogany dining table contained ten leaves. The chairs were of finely tooled leather. He tried to relax, to reassure himself. He would not have been promoted had it not been felt he could handle the job. He had been knighted for his bravery in battle. Sir Raymond Knight, Knight of the Bath. His name and title had been the object of wardroom humor on more than one occasion. Unconsciously, he touched his neck which caused him to wince. The burn had just about healed, leaving the skin thickened and scarred and somewhat darkened. The burn had reached from his neck down to his chest and upper arm. Wearing his uniform made matters even worse. On board *LeFrelon*, he never wore his coat, except as specifically required by duty. An outcry of laughter broke Knight's revive. Someone must have said something very amusing to cause such an outcry. Looking up Knight noticed a young, tall, dark-complected lieutenant approaching him.

"I'm Gabe," the lieutenant said by way of introduction as he held out his hand. "Looks like Lieutenant Kerry is catching the devil from Lieutenant Bush," Gabe said addressing the laughter.

"Aye," Knight replied. "I'm told they're related so no doubt the banter is friendly."

Shaking Knight's hand Gabe saw him wince and regretted his momentary absence of mind. However, other than the quick involuntary reaction, Knight gave no other hint of what he must be feeling. Gabe quickly looked at the tall prematurely graying man and decided instantly that he liked him. Knight had given a firm handshake with a quick smile on his face to cover the pain he had felt.

"I understand it was you who captured *LeFrelon*," Knight said. "I'm grateful, she's a good sailor."

Feeling a bit embarrassed, Gabe corrected the commander, "I was supernumerary on the ship that took *LeFrelon*. It was actually Lieutenant Markham commanding *Swan* that took her."

"Don't you believe a word of that, sir." This from Markham who had been standing close and overhearing the conversation joined in. "No sir, it was Lieutenant Anthony alone. A cutlass in his teeth and a pistol in each hand he laid about the damn privateer like a man crazed. Hacking and cutting his way through the cutthroats with cannon's thundering, blades clinging and musket ball flying through the air like a hive of bees."

"Were you not wounded, sir?" Knight asked Gabe thoughtfully.

Before Gabe could answer, Markham continued, "Wounded…wounded you ask? Well, hell no. He was killed. Killed dead, sir, I swear, didn't you know like a cat, Gabe's got nine lives."

As Markham finished his outlandish tale the group of officers howled with laughter. Smiling in spite of being the brunt of Markham's joke, Knight thought again, *no sir, these men were nothing like those commanded by Commodore Meriwether.*

CLINK…CLINK…CLINK… Captain Buck, Lord Anthony's flag captain, overhearing Markham's narrative tried to compose himself as he tapped a wine glass with a spoon. A concerned Silas, the admiral's cook, sat in the corner. He was tempted to take the spoon out of the captain's hand. That wine glass was crystal and if Buck broke it with that damn spoon Lady Deborah would never forgive him.

The group quieted down and much to Silas's relief Buck laid the spoon down. "Gentlemen," Buck spoke to the room at large, "His Lordship was detained at the meeting with the Governor as you were all told, but his barge is approaching. Not a minute too soon I'm thinking as his generosity with a canter of wine appears to have taken on broader proportions. I hope there's sufficient left that Silas won't have to go ashore before Lord Anthony can have his supper."

This brought chuckles from the officers. When Lord Anthony came aboard he went directly to his dining room and addressed the issues that had been discussed at the Governor's meeting. He also outlined his plan of action and it was a determined group that returned to their ships.

"Like old times is it not?" Markham said to Earl. "Pair up and patrol."

"Aye," a smiling Earl responded. "I just hope we're as lucky with a prize or two as his lordship was when we were in the West Indies."

"Aye," Markham replied, his mind already on how much his share would be as a ship's captain compared to when he was a midshipman.

The wind came from the north-northwest. Lord Anthony had shifted his flag to *Merlin* leaving his flag lieutenant, a disappointed and spitting-'n'-sputtering Captain Buck, behind on *HMS Warrior*. While *Warrior* was a fine third rate, she was much too big and cumbersome for the patrol Lord Anthony had in mind. *Warrior* made a fine sight lying at anchor where just the threat of her guns would ward off most attempts to invade Saint Augustine. But *Warrior* would not serve well in the Keys. "We need smaller ships with shallow droughts to get in among the Keys as we patrol south along Florida's coast," he explained. He had also left the ketch, *HMS Pigeon*, and the cutter, *HMS Audacity*, as Anthony wanted this to be a quick patrol and they'd never be able to keep up. Sailing as close to the coast as they were the bluish water was almost clear and alive with all types of fish. Gulls filled the air; the gawking birds would spread their wings and hover in the air. Then, off they'd go, harrying other birds that came into their space.

A group of off watch seamen had fashioned fishing lines and one had caught a nice size red snapper. As he was pulling the fish in a barracuda flashed by. His body like silver daggers as he bit the snapper into, leaving the fisherman with only the head for his troubles.

Bart, standing alongside Lord Anthony and *Merlin's* captain, Stephen Earl, had watched the scene as it had taken place in the clear water. "Makes you think about wot Gabe reported don't it?" Bart volunteered. "That frigate just tearing apart the brig the way he did. No conscience, that bugger, a vicious one I'm thinking."

Used to Bart's uncanny ability to bring one's thoughts to bear, Anthony agreed. "He's vicious no doubt, but what would cause a man to be so?"

"Are you thinking we could be dealing with Montique, my Lord?"

"No, Stephen. Montique would have sunk the ship, but he would have taken off everything of value before doing so. I think we're dealing with a different type villain this time."

"Deck there!" The lookout called, "A signal from *HMS SeaWolf*, sail in sight."

"Have Gabe investigate," a visibly excited Anthony ordered Earl. "Then signal *LeFrelon* to assist."

"Aye, my Lord," Earl replied but before he could give his orders the lookout called down again.

"*SeaWolf*'as signaled three sails from the sou'west."

"Damme, but this may be a profitable day," Earl exclaimed unable to keep the excitement from his voice.

Once Earl had gone about his duties, Bart edged up to Lord Anthony. "We's a fight ahead o' us today. I feel hit in me bones. No sightseers today I'm thinking."

"Why you damned old bilge rat," Anthony retorted, "I bet you don't even know where your blade is and if you do, I'll bet the blade has rusted in the scabbard."

"Aye, it may be with us standing 'bout all da time but I's betting Silas has got some slush wot'll free it up, and hit ain't too late to put a new edge on it."

"Sail ho! Three sails in sight. Two be schooner and one be a bigger fish."

Hearing this Earl looked at Anthony and rolled his eyes, "Gawd," he groaned and called to the first lieutenant, "take a glass to the mast, Mr. Rodney, and tell us what you see. Damme man, his Lordship is right over there, do I have to remind you of your duties in front of the admiral?"

A sheepish Bart turned to larboard to hide his grin as he whispered to Anthony, "Earl's a cheeky bugger, ain't he?   Sounds like Captain Buck when he says 'Gawd' don't he?"

Trying not to chuckle, Anthony replied, "Aye, that he does, but let's go below and let Captain Earl run his ship."

Chapter Seven

Gabe stood perched against the forward bulwark, glass to his eye. He braced himself to get a better view as *SeaWolf* plunged through another wave. The dip and roll made it difficult to focus on the approaching ships. Two schooners and a small frigate. The schooners were clearly a pair of Jonathan's but the frigate…he couldn't be sure…probably Spanish, but not the same one that had blasted the brig a few days back.

Another dip of *SeaWolf's* bow allowed a cresting wave to come aboard, fairly drenching Gabe then running down the scuppers. *Damn*, Gabe said to himself somewhat embarrassed. He'd been so focused on the approaching sails he'd not paid attention and now was paying the price.

"Decided to take a bath did you?" Dagan asked. It was what the first lieutenant had wanted to ask but didn't, not yet sure of his relationship with the captain.

Glaring at Dagan, Gabe snapped, "It's a warm day, why not?"

Dagan not moved by Gabe's attempt at sternness asked cheerfully, "Should I have Lum bring you some soap or will a towel do?"

Unable to act irritated any longer Gabe said, "A towel will do."

The sun shone bright on the sparkling water. Little vapors were seen arising from Gabe's uniform as he gave his hands and face a final rub with the towel. "Make a signal to the flag, Mr. Lancaster, three privateer, two schooners and one frigate of twenty-eight guns."

"Aye, cap'n," the youth responded then hurried off to do his bidding before the cap'n caught him smiling.

Turning to the first lieutenant, Gabe asked, "Where lies *LeFrelon?*"

"She's overreaching us now, sir," Lavery volunteered before Jackson could speak.

"Very well. Beat to quarters, Mr. Jackson. I feel it will be two against three until *Merlin* can overhaul us."

"Think we could delay things until she arrives?" Jackson asked not liking the odds of two large schooners of fourteen guns each and the twenty-eight gun frigate. It was more than any sane man would want to face.

"I don't think it's up to us," Gabe replied, noting the privateers had split up. The two schooners to windward and the frigate to leeward.

"Bet they've played this game before," Gunnells offered.

"Deck there! Signal from *LeFrelon*. Attack ships to windward."

After pausing, Gabe realized Knight was the senior of the two so he had the right to give Gabe orders. *He will have a hard time of it*, Gabe thought. It was apparent Knight was no coward or one to shirk his duty. He'd taken the frigate leaving Gabe with the schooners, theoretically a more even match up.

"*Merlin* has signaled, harass the enemy," Jackson said.

"What's he mean?" Dagan, who had been listening but had not spoken, now addressed the first lieutenant.

"His way of telling us to be careful if possible. Harass, but don't attack. If we can play cat 'n' mouse long enough, we'll have the odds in our favor."

"I wish the admiral hadn't sent *Swan* off on dispatch," Lavery interjected.

"Not squeamish are you sir?" Gunnells asked. Being new on board *SeaWolf*, the master had no idea of the action Lavery had been in.

Hearing the interaction, Gabe not wanting any conflict spoke up for his lieutenant, "Nay, Lavery's not squeamish. Prudent is more to my thinking."

"Deck there, the leading schooner 'as opened 'er gunports," the lookout called down.

"No doubt now," Gabe volunteered to his officers. "They are deliberately seeking action." After looking over the ship Gabe spoke to the first lieutenant, Mr. Jackson. "Those boarding nets are too tight. See to them if you will sir, they need to be slackened."

Then looking down the main deck he could see the gun crews were standing about. The gunner had already carefully selected his first ball, making sure it was free of any rust and as near perfect as could be for roundness. The men had various types of scarves and bandanas tied over their ears to reduce the noise.

A tub full of cutlasses, pikes and boarding axes set amidship. Turning aft Gabe saw Lum and Dawkins. Neither had to be involved but he'd not try to talk them into going below to safety. Dagan was aft as well; he was talking to Caleb.

Wonder where that damned ape is, Gabe thought. As the thought crossed his mind so did another. Dagan was making his way toward him so Gabe held his thought. When Dagan grew close he spoke softly, "Did you ever hear of an ape being killed in action?"

Dagan stopped dead in his tracks and looked directly into Gabe's eyes then they both burst out in laughter.

One of the gun captains hearing the laughter spoke to his gun crew, "Lookie there laddies, iffen the cap'n can 'ave 'isself a chuckle then he can't be much worried about them buggers. So when the ossifer gives the word, fire, let's lay about like I's done showed ya!"

The gun captain was a leathered wrinkled old salt who was nearly deaf from serving the guns for thirty or more years. His ready grin showed gaps between his yellowed teeth. Experienced as he was, his word put not only his gun crew but also those on either side at ease.

BOOM!...BOOM!...BOOM!

"Well, they'd open the ball," Gunnells cried out.

Gabe ignored the privateer's opening shots. They were more for effect that anything else. It would be another five minutes before they would be in effect range. Noticing how the two schooners were sailing gave Gabe an idea. It would be nip 'n' tuck for a harried moment or so, but he knew what *SeaWolf* could do.

"Mr. Gunnells, do you see the two schooners are running parallel but the lead ship has a good distance over the sister ship?"

"Aye, cap'n, I sees it."

"I want to split the two, then come around and pour a broadside up the latter ship's bunghole."

Smiling, Gunnells replied, "I'll lay her so close to yonder ship's stern you could walk through the galley windows if you've a mind."

"No nothing that close," Gabe answered the old master, "But pistol shot range will do."

BOOM!...BOOM!

"The frigate has fired on *LeFrelon*," the lookout called.

Smoke had engulfed the privateer momentarily but was now drifting between the two ships.

BOOM!...BOOM!

The roar of cannon filled the air as *LeFrelon* fired back scoring a hit as pieces of debris went flying into the air. Seeing this, Gabe called to his gun crews, "A guinea to the first gun to score a hit."

This brought cheers from the men, profit and a gut full-o'-glory, "Huzza to the cap'n, huzza."

"Open ports," Gabe ordered Jackson.

"Mr. Druett," Gabe called to his gunner, "Let go with the bowchaser if you will. I want those rogues to feel *SeaWolf's* fangs."

"Aye, cap'n. Hear that lads," Druett called. "Time for *SeaWolf* to bare her fangs and give them whoresons a bite or two."

BOOM!...BOOM! Both nine pounders had fired.

"We claim the guinea," a man cried. Sure enough the huge jib on the leading schooner had been hit causing her to skew to larboard.

"Foul! Foul," the ole gapped-tooth gun captain cried. "We've had no chance to bear."

Raising his hands in surrender, "Fair is fair," Gabe called. "We'll make it even. A guinea to the first crew on each side to score a hit, but a tie means you split the purse."

This brought more cheers from the men. *SeaWolf* was now bearing down on the schooners.

As an afterthought, Gabe turned to Jackson, "Are the boats being towed?"

"Aye, captain, I set Mr. Graf to it soon as you ordered beat to quarters."

SeaWolf and the leading schooner were virtually parallel. As Gabe gave the order to fire he could hear the firing as *LeFrelon* battled her foe. Lanyards jerked as one as the anxious gun captains heard the order they'd been waiting on.

SeaWolf rocked back as a whole broadside let loose with a tremendous crash. The entire side was in a frenzy.

As the guns hurled backwards to the end of their breechings, clouds of dirty yellow 'n' black acrid smoke filled the air then flowed aft toward the quarterdeck with the breeze.

The gun crew flung themselves at their guns as the gun captains shouted instructions and encouragement.

"Worm out, worm out laddies. 'At's it, now swab. Atkins, ya bugger I said swab."

Worming, swabbing, reloading, and running out, each crew was like a well-oiled machine. The occasional curse from a gun captain was more for show than need.

"Lively now!   Fire! That's it, you lubberly whoresons! Worm…swab…reload." On and on it went, each crew trying to beat the time of the next crew.

Gabe tried to watch the fall of shot. The schooner was being pounded but *SeaWolf* was being hit as well. Several gaps were in the bulwark, the forward mainsail had a huge rent and one gun was overturned. One of the gun crew lay beneath the heavy barrel, his legs kicking the air. Then mercifully they thudded to the deck and lay still. Then they were past the first ship. Would he come about or continue on? Gabe wasn't sure but if things worked to plan, he'd have the second schooner between them.

"He's trying to come about, sir." This from Gunnells, "He's trying to come about on the same tack."

Well, he couldn't worry about that now; they were along side the other schooner and *SeaWolf* rocked as she was racked by the privateer's broadside.

"Four pounders," Jackson cried out, "She's only got four pounders."

Was he glad or complaining, Dagan wondered. *SeaWolf* rocked again but this time it was from her own broadside. The schooner was hit good, but was firing her guns again, those that were left after *SeaWolf* spoke.

"She's got a good skipper," Gabe spoke to Dagan.

"Aye, he's making a fight of it."

Gabe had made his way aft to Gunnells and the wheel. He looked at the schooner as *SeaWolf* slid by then after a pause bellowed his order. "Now, Mr. Gunnells, down helm. Put your helm down."

The master had two men at the wheel. With all their might they spun the big wheel. Gabe felt the rudder bite and *SeaWolf* made her turn to larboard bringing the loaded cannon to bear on the stern.

"Ease her up, that's it, ease her up," Gabe ordered.

SeaWolf crossed the privateer's stern with each gun firing as they sailed past. The galley windows were shattered by the first gun with each subsequent shot lending to the destruction of the one before it.

Then there was an explosion as the magazine was undoubtedly hit. The once proud beautiful ship was now nothing by fiery debris filling the air, then raining down all about. Huge chunks were hitting the sea with splashing and sizzling sounds.

Suddenly, one of the worst sounds heard aboard ship rang out: "Fire! Fire! Fire to the mainsail."

Gabe turned to Gunnells, "Put the ship before the wind, then heave to." He then shouted orders to Jackson, "Clew up the topsail and top gallant. Then cut away the mainsail."

"Lavery?"

"Aye, captain."

"Get a bucket line formed."

"Graf?"

"Aye, sir."

"Get the hammocks and blankets soaked and ready if we need them."

"Mr. Dover?"

"Here, sir," the carpenter answered.

"Open the sea-cock and get some water in the bilges, then get the ship's pumps ready. Hopefully we won't need them, but let's get them ready."

"Aye, cap'n." As the carpenter turned to carry out his duties Gabe called after him again.

"Mr. Dover."

"Sir."

"Don't forget to close the sea-cocks. We want to put water in the bilge, not sink the ship."

"Aye, sir, close them I will."

Dagan then sidled up to Gabe, "Here comes the other privateer."

"Damme," Gabe said, not liking the thought of having to surrender.

BOOM!…BOOM!…Gabe looked for the fall of the shot not seeing any damage to *SeaWolf*.

"Look sir," one of the petty officers called out, "It's *Merlin*. She's firing on the privateer."

"Huzzah! Huzzah for the *Merlin*," *SeaWolf's* crew cheered.

On board *Merlin*, Lord Anthony and Bart watched as *SeaWolf's* crew fought the flames. Meanwhile, Earl guided his ship into combat against the remaining schooner. *LeFrelon* and the privateering frigate were locked together and were in hand-to-hand combat.

"We's got to 'urry," Bart volunteered, "else Knight and his bunch'll be overrun."

Lord Anthony was also concerned. He wanted to help Gabe but he also had to go to Knight's aid. However, the damnable schooner came first.

"Captain Earl?"

"Aye, my Lord."

"I'd be grateful if your next salvo was double-shotted with a measure of grape. Time is of the essence."

Earl understood the urgency and had himself been torn between which ship to aid. *In theory, Gabe should be able to handle the fire but...*

The cannons had been loaded as ordered and after coming about *Merlin* unleashed its deadly broadside. The weight of its metal stopped the schooner dead in the water. The once proud schooner should have hauled her wind after the first exchange with *Merlin's* bigger twelve pounder cannons.

The ship was mastless, and pockmarked from the stern forward. Men were scurrying to abandon ship as the schooner was already down forward.

"Come about if you will, sir," Lord Anthony was addressing Earl. "Let's see if we can lie alongside the rogue," he continued, using his sword as a pointer. "Pray to God we're not too late."

As *Merlin* approached the privateer frigate men started firing muskets and swivels in their direction. One of the men at the wheel involuntarily let up, as a ball hit the deck next to him.

"Steer small, blast you," *Merlin's* master hissed at the man. *Merlin* yawed then was instantly corrected.

The frigate's transom was now level with *Merlin's* jib boom. A heavy thump, then the scraping and grinding of wood as the two ships came together.

"Boarders away, boarders away," Earl was calling when he saw Bart and Lord Anthony, pistol in one hand and blade in the other.

"My Lord," he cried, "It's not for you to be boarding, sir."

Touched, but not amazed at Earl's sincerity, Anthony answered, "I must lead by example Stephen, you most of all should realize that."

"Aye, my Lord," Earl muttered as he stepped aside.

"Don't yew worry none, cap'n," Bart spoke as he passed, "I's protecting 'im."

"Humph! You can't protect yourself so how are you to protect me?" Anthony asked.

"I's will, don't yews be worrying how, jus' knows I will."

The flash of powder as muskets and pistols fired continued all around. Realizing they were now being assaulted on two fronts the privateers were now fighting like madmen. Cutlasses flashed amid cries of anguish and pain. Bart discharged his pistol into a man's rotund belly as the man jabbed at Lord Anthony with a boarding pike.

Earl aimed at what appeared to be an officer and squeezed the trigger. As the man went down he put the fired pistol in his waistband and shifted his other pistol to his right hand. When he spotted another target, he aimed, held his breath for a second then fired. When the second man collapsed he took his sword and joined into the fight.

The privateers were now tiring. They'd all but won the battle with *LeFrelon* when *Merlin* joined in. A small half-crazed man screaming profanities was skewered by Lord Anthony's blade. He dropped the axe he had been carrying and bolted toward a ladder, before dropping to the deck, letting out a final bloodcurdling profane scream.

Earl, who was by Lord Anthony looked at the admiral and declared, "Blasphemy, by Gawd."

"Damnation," Bart cried. "Look!"

Knight was in the midst of a melee. The man could be heard yelling encouragement to his men. His voice strong and commanding could be heard above the din of battle.

Dead and dying men lay sprawled about the deck. Little knots of men were still fighting. Lord Anthony now was face to face with a man carrying a blade and a tomahawk. Desperation showed on the man's face and eyes as he circled and prodded with his blade, feinting then swinging the tomahawk.

Circling with the man, Anthony became aware of how slick the deck had become from all the blood and gore. Feeling himself tire, Anthony knew he had to soon end it. Then just as he started to press the man, there was a loud crack to his left.

His opponent's face turned from that of a man to unrecognizable gore. As the man dropped to the deck Bart stepped up next to Lord Anthony, smoking pistol still in his hand.

"No need to bother with that bugger. Iffen he'd 'ad any sense he'd throwed down 'is weapons and surrendered proper like. 'Nother one o' them buggers wot shoulda learned 'scretion, I'm thinking. Now 'e'll never share another wet with 's mates."

The fighting was now over. *Merlin's* marine lieutenant was bellowing at his men to form up. Wounded men were being carried below and the bodies of dead privateers were being dumped unceremoniously overboard. Cries from the orlop deck could be heard as Bart and Lord Anthony made their way back on board *Merlin*.

Turning to Lord Anthony, Bart spoke in a very solemn voice, "I don't know wot's worse, dying on deck or at the 'ands o' the surgeon."

Nursing a cut arm, Anthony replied, "I don't know but I think it's quicker in battle."

"Aye," Bart agreed, "Plus yew don't 'ave to lay there and think on it."

Back on board *SeaWolf*, Gabe and his crew were able to get the burning sail cut away and overboard before the fire had spread. Most of the damage from the battle was to the rails and bulwark. One gun would have to have a new carriage. Two crewmembers were dead and several wounded, a few from fighting the fire and not the battle.

LeFrelon was not so lucky. She had twenty dead and twice that wounded. The ship had taken a beating and may sink.

"Several planks has been stove in," the carpenter reported, "Plus she be holed twice."

As Knight reported to Admiral Anthony he felt distraught. "I doubt she'll ever fight again, my Lord. The frigate's heavier guns pounded her badly, I'm afraid."

"Think she'll make it to Saint Augustine?" Anthony inquired.

"I'm not sure, my Lord. If the wind doesn't get up she might."

"Very well," Lord Anthony said with a sigh. "Leave your first lieutenant and a skeleton crew on board and you take command of the frigate. What was her name?" Anthony asked.

"The *Neptune*, sir."

"Ah, yes, the *Neptune*. Since Lord Howe has promoted you to commander of *LeFrelon*, I'm sure he'll confirm your promotion to captain and command of the frigate. Did you loose any officers?"

"No, my Lord."

"Good, then we'll do what we can for *LeFrelon* now, and make a final decision when we get back to Saint Augustine."

PART II

Skylarking

Searching for fresh air.
The crew gathering on deck,
And stared out in awe;
As the Caribbean sun set.
They drank down their ration,
And lit up their pipes.
The master had promised,
Another scorching night.

-Michael Aye

Chapter Eight

The weeks following the battle with the privateers proved to be less rewarding. It was monotonous at times and hot all the time.

Anthony sent the ships out on patrol in pairs. *Merlin* and *Swan* were plying the coast up to Wilmington, North Carolina where two transports had been taken by rebel gunboats.

The Cape Fear River poured out into the Atlantic at Wilmington. The area had over a dozen inlets and most were suited for privateering. Strike fast, then escape into one of the inlets where navigation would be very treacherous for someone who didn't know the area.

Captain Knight on the newly captured *Neptune*, and Gabe on *SeaWolf* had just returned from their patrol south to the Keys and back. *Pigeon* and *Audacity* took turns as transport from the anchorage to Saint Augustine. *Warrior* continued at anchorage providing protection to the city.

"Boat ahoy!" Anthony could hear the challenge through the open skylight. A few minutes later Buck came down.

"Sir, flag captain," the marine sentry announced.

As Captain Buck entered, Anthony called to Silas, "Bring us a glass of hock if you will."

"Aye, my Lord, I have to fetch it from the bilges, but it shouldn't take long."

Seeing the official envelope with the Governor's seal, Anthony asked, "What have we here?"

"I'd guess it's an invitation," Buck replied.

"To what?"

"You'll have to tell me sir, as it's addressed to you."

Anthony tore open the seal, and then sat silent for a moment while he read the invitation. "Well, Rupert," he spoke to Buck, using his first name. "It's time for you to meet some of the city's more eligible ladies."

"I don't understand," Buck said with a slight frown across his brow.

"The Governor is having a ball. Why, I have no idea, but you and the other ship's captains are all invited. As I recall, it was at such an affair you struck up quite a relationship with a lady on Antigua."

"Aye," Buck replied as a smile creased his face. "A most warm and loving lady she was until she found out I'd not quit the sea to become her kept man. Mind you now, it was like a honeymoon itself every time we came back into port," Buck continued as he recalled the buxom dark-haired woman who had offered him a life of luxury.

"Trouble was, sir, nothing went with it. The plantation stayed in her name. She didn't want marriage and I couldn't see myself as some nabob."

Anthony couldn't help but chuckle. He and Buck had been together for a long time and he could just see him as some rich widow's kept man.

"Wouldn't mind seeing her again for a day or so. Then I'd be ready to set sail," Buck said as he took a deep sigh.

"Well, we'll see if Saint Augustine has anyone to stir your humours."

"Huh!" Buck replied. "There's plenty of that, I don't know if it's the sun or possibly the Spanish heritage sir, but the women in the…ah…establishments around Saint Augustine are dark-skinned with ready smiles and bold looks. The way they flash their eyes at you is enough to set a sailor's heart ablaze. They tend to be very shapely, sir, all buxom and smiles. Several of our lads wouldn't mind having a closer relationship with the local women I'm told."

"Well," Anthony said as he pushed his chair back allowing Silas to pour the hock he'd retrieved from the bilges, "let's try not to cause any problems with the local men over these women."

"Nay, my lord, there'll be no trouble as long as our jack tars keep a full purse and a condom on hand."

Admiral Lord Anthony walked down the corridor toward the ballroom; Flag Captain Buck at his side and Flag Lieutenant Hazard was directly behind. As the door was opened by a footman Anthony heard Hazard take in a deep breath when he saw the bare shoulders and deep cleavages of the ladies who were wearing gowns of various colors. Anthony saw Buck hesitate ever so slightly in his pace so that Hazard would come abreast then whispered to the lieutenant, "Don't stare." Hazard gulped and shook his head.

Buck then leaned toward Anthony and spoke softly, "Not as grand as Antigua but the evening has promise."

As the three officers made their way further through the entrance and to the first step of three that led down to the ballroom floor the footman tapped a long stave on the floor gaining everyone's attention, "Admiral Lord Gilbert Anthony."

This drew curious stares from the mass of people already circulating inside the ballroom. A huge chandelier hung in the middle of the ceiling with four smaller ones bordering it. The heat from the candles intensified the already warm evening. The musicians as if on cue started playing again.

The governor, looking debonair, was dressed in all white much as he had been when Anthony first met him.

Anthony introduced Captain Buck and said, "You remember my Flag Lieutenant Everette Hazard?"

Greetings were exchanged and the Governor said, "I have someone I'd like you to meet, my Lord."

This was Buck and Hazard's cue for each to go their separate way. Hazard looked somewhat lost but was quickly relieved when he spotted other naval officers he knew. Buck had spotted a lady who had on such a low cut gown she need not have covered herself at all. She returned Buck's bold stare then flashed a fan to her face trying to hide a glint of a smile as Buck made his way toward her. *Maybe the evening holds more than just promise,* Buck thought.

Buck took one glance over his shoulder and saw Anthony and the Governor shaking hands with another man.

"Lord Anthony, I'd like you to meet Colonel Thomas Browne," Governor Tonyn said as he introduced the two men. "As I've placed the defense of Florida in your capable hands I thought the two of you should meet. I have given Colonel Browne command of the Florida rangers."

"How many men do you have?" Anthony asked.

"At present we have two hundred or so," Browne answered, "but the way…we fight large numbers would only work against us. My rangers are made up of Seminole Indians led by Chief Cowcatcher, loyalist and free black men who know their way around the woods."

Listening to the man talk Anthony could feel his energy and knew right away he was a very competent soldier. Browne soon excused himself as he was summoned by a very attractive lady.

As he made his departure Tonyn stepped close to Anthony and said, "Would you believe the damn Georgia rebels tarred, feathered and partially scalped Browne? That's why his hair is long."

Seeing a British officer Tonyn said, "That's General Augustin Prevost, Commander of the Royal American Regiment. He is in charge of the defense of Saint Augustine. As you can imagine, he doesn't like Colonel Browne. He doesn't think Browne's guerrilla warfare is honorable. Not a gentleman, he says." But speaking very stern Tonyn said, "For what the rebels send against us I'd rather have Browne's rangers than a dozen of Prevost's regiments."

As the evening continued Anthony spied Hazard and one of Knight's lieutenants standing in the center of a group of young ladies. Seeing the smiles on the lieutenant's faces and the look of awe from the young ladies he could only imagine what tale of derring-do's was being told.

Without realizing her actions, one young lady touched Hazard's empty sleeve. The young lieutenant was so enthralled with the conversation he appeared not to have noticed the act, something that would have caused him to jerk back three months ago.

Good, thought Anthony. *He's realizing the loss of the arm didn't make him less of a man. He at this particular time appeared to be treated like the hero he was.*

Anthony continued to observe the group a few more minutes when he realized how much he missed Lady Deborah...Lady Deborah and a daughter he'd yet to lay eyes on. *Damn this war*, he thought, *damn it to hell.*

Chapter Nine

Gabe was listening to the sounds overhead as he sipped on his coffee. Lum seemed awkward this morning, almost distant.

"Did you enjoy your time ashore last night?" Gabe asked. Dawkins had taken Lum in tow and the two had gone into Saint Augustine.

"Yes, suh."

"What did you think of the town," Gabe asked trying to draw Lum into conversation.

"Well, suh, Beaufort ain't got nuthin' on it, but it ain't no Charlestown." Lum still wasn't his usual self.

"Is there a problem Lum?" Gabe asked.

"Well, suh, I jus' ain't used being round no trouble."

At that time there was a knock at the cabin door. "First lieutenant, sir," the sentry said.

As Jackson made his way in Gabe could feel his stomach tighten. The look on Jackson's face was enough.

"What is it Mr. Jackson?"

"Mr. Lancaster is in jail, sir."

"In jail, damme sir, what's this about?" Gabe exclaimed.

"He was in an altercation at some tavern."

"The Mermaid," Lum volunteered. Both officers turned to look at Lum.

"You know about this?"

"Aye, sir, I was there."

"Is this the trouble you just spoke of?"

"Yas suh, that's hit."

"Well what happened?" Gabe asked.

"Well suh, Dawkins, he done struck up a conversation wid what he called a lovely little doxy. Deys was two of dem, but old Lum didn't wants ta boder wid 'em none cause I's be thinking about Missy Faith and Nanny. Well, upstairs Dawkins goes whilst I watch over his purse and finish my wet. Den da's a comotion to beat da devil. Dis sodjar man trys to kiss Mistah Lancaster on da face. Den Mistah Lancaster slaps dat sodjar man a good'un and says he don't have no time fah no damn sodimite sodjar. Dat heathen then grabs a-hole of Mistah Lancaster like he was a woman and say's 'When I'm done ye'll be squealing like a pig.' "

"When Mistah Lancaster wouldn't squeal da man starts biting on his eah and foh ya know'd it he done bit poh Mistah Lancaster's eah clean off. Dat's when Mistah Lancaster felt blood running down his face and puts his hand to his eah but dey ain't no eah dar, so he cries out 'You bung bustin' scum' and shoots da man right in his...his...ah...you knows what Bart calls 'is wedding tackle. Den da's dis Captain man wid moh sodjars take poh Mistah Lancaster off to da jail."

Gabe and Jackson sat astonished at Lum's narrative. "And you saw it all?" Gabe finally asked.

"Aye, suh, wid my own peepers. I's as close as I is to you right now."

"Well, I'd better go check on our midshipman. Mr. Jackson, get my gig ready," Gabe said. "Where's Dagan?"

"I'm here," Dagan called. He had slipped in and poured himself a cup of coffee as Lum had told his story.

"Where have you been?" Gabe asked Dagan.

"With Dawkins, he was roughed up a bit afterwards by a provost sergeant of the sixtieth when he went to check on Lancaster. Lum laid the sergeant out and brought Dawkins back to the ship. He's with Caleb now. Caleb says he'll be fine."

Turning back to Lum, Gabe said, "Is there more?"

"Not much, suh. We went to check on Mistah Lancaster adder Dawkins finished his business wid that little doxy. Dat sergeant acted real uppity like and said they'd handle the little sailor boy. Dawkins den told the man he'd be back and they'd see who handled whom. When Dawkins turned to go dats when dat sodjar hit him wid 'is pistol so I jus' clops dat man a good'un and down he wents."

"What did you hit him with?" Gabe asked.

Lum looked sheepish as he replied, "Dawkins bottle 'od kill devil."

"Did the sergeant see you?" Gabe asked.

"No suh, not lessen 'e's got eyes in da back o' 'is head and iffen he do I 'speck they's busted."

Lord Anthony was discussing the ball from the previous evening with Buck. He told of his meeting Colonel Browne, and then asked Buck how his evening had gone, expecting a lewd tale. Bart was expecting some bawdy tale as well as he continued to hang around the pantry when normally he'd be out and about.

Buck had just started when through the skylight the challenge "boat ahoy!"

SeaWolf came the response. While Gabe and Lord Anthony were brothers it was only upon invitation Gabe would visit the flagship.

"I'll go," Buck said then grabbed his hat and headed topside.

Later in Lord Anthony's cabin Gabe retold Lum's story as he'd just told Buck. "When I went to the jail a provost major told me pretty quick Lancaster was under arrest for attempted murder and I didn't have the authority to have him released or to even see him for that matter. Said he was tired of the Navy acting like they owned the damn city. He did tell me, Lancaster would be tried tomorrow and likely be hanged by sunset."

Hearing this Lord Anthony stood up suddenly and said, "Nay! There'll be no hanging unless it's that damnable sodimite. Bart?"

"I's getting the barge ready now sir," Bart said, not needing to be told.

"Captain Buck, I'm going to the governor's; meanwhile you take marine Captain Dunlap and a squad of his men to the jail. Tell that popinjay major I'd consider it a compliment if he'd release Lancaster into your custody."

"Aye," Buck replied, "and if he don't I'll have Dunlap shoot the bastard."

The governor was out when Anthony arrived unannounced.

"His Excellency is expected soon, my Lord," Tonyn's secretary assured Anthony, not quite sure what to do with someone of Lord Anthony's status. Finally, he said, "May I offer you some refreshment while you wait, my Lord?"

Tonyn had just returned and was in the process of greeting Anthony when the sound of horses could be heard and a coach slid to a halt causing a grinding sound on the flagstones outside the governor's door. In came General Prevost puffing and all in a flush. Ignoring protocol he shouted, "Damme, man, what type of a fool are you to send a post captain and a squad of marines to take a prisoner from my jail?"

Anthony took a step forward and spoke with a grimace, "I'll lay your current actions to the heat outside sir, but take notice, you ever speak to me in that tone again I'll have satisfaction. I'm told you are a gentleman so I'm sure you know what I mean. Now as to your accusations, sir, I sent a post captain to give my compliments to your provost asking for the accused to be released into my custody. The marines were to escort the accused back aboard ship."

Realizing he was on dangerous ground with a man who was no stranger to death the general took a deep breath and stammered, "Put that way sir, I see no reason the prisoner shouldn't be released to you as long as he's returned to appear before a court martial."

"On whose authority will the court martial be convened," Anthony challenged.

Realizing things could get very sticky the governor said, "The incident took place in a civil establishment, therefore, it will be a civil matter and I will appoint the judge."

Glaring, the general said, "Very well."

"As it should be," Tonyn stated.

The general then turned on his heels and left.

"You've made an enemy there," Tonyn addressed the admiral after the general was out the door.

"Not the first, nor likely the last," Anthony replied, then thanked the governor for his intervention and departed.

The Mermaid was a square, low ceiling room with open shutters so sunlight would fill the otherwise dimly lit taproom. A short staircase led to a second floor door, probably the tavern keeper's sleeping quarters or rooms used by the doxies to entertain.

As he turned, Gabe saw a scorched fireplace across the room from a half circle bar. The bar showed signs of age and scars from many drunken brawls. The tavern keeper was there leaning on the bar with his elbows. His shirt had once been white but was now stained to a deep yellow. His sleeves were rolled up showing strong arms. He was short and had an immense rotund belly, probably from sampling his wares Gabe thought.

Straightening up the man smiled and said, "Greetings señor. It is not often we get such an honoured patron." He had recognized Gabe as an officer. He extended a meaty hand toward Gabe and said, "I'm Domingo Chavez."

Gabe liked the little man. As he reached forward to shake the offered hand the man's small mouth broke out in a smile revealing brown tobacco stained teeth.

"You are not with the Army, señor?' Chavez asked.

"No, I'm in the Navy," Gabe answered.

"Always, I've wanted to see what it would be like to be on a ship at sea. But alas, you see that I cannot," Chavez said as he stretched out his arms and gave a shrug. "Always, I'm here. This place has been in my family before the Spanish left. Now there are only a few of us but I could not leave what was my father's. But you did not come to hear about Domingo, what is it I can do for you señor?"

"I want to know about a soldier," Gabe replied, "The bully who hurt the boy."

"Si, I know him. He always makes trouble. He likes to bust up things but never likes to pay for damages. He got what he asked for."

"Would you be willing to testify to that?" Gabe asked.

"No, señor, to do so would mean death. My place would burn, my family hurt. No, señor, I cannot."

"I will pay you for the bar and I will provide protection," Gabe replied, "For you and your family." Gabe watched the man thinking it over.

"I would have to know who it was that would protect me and perhaps we could be partners, eh señor?"

"Fine," Gabe said, "Let's agree on price and I will send you money for the partnership with the man who will protect you."

Chavez looked skeptical as he spoke, "Only one man, señor?"

"Aye," Gabe replied, "His name is Dagan."

"What about papers señor? Do we have to have documents drawn up?"

Gabe paused and looked at the man, "Is your handshake not good enough?"

"Si, señor, Domingo's word is as good as gold."

"Then we don't need any papers," Gabe said as he departed.

Chapter Ten

Sir Raymond Knight sat at his desk going over the notes he had made while talking to all concerned parties in the assault case against Midshipman Lancaster. By concerned parties, he meant Lancaster, Lum and Domingo Chavez.

Knight had talked to a number of soldiers who were known to have been in the bar at the time of the incident. However, none claimed to have seen or heard anything out of the ordinary. Giving a sigh, Knight pushed his chair back and thinking aloud said, "Well, it don't help none but it don't hurt us either."

It all boiled down to how well the three did being cross examined by the provost marshal. Lum was the key. If he did well Lancaster would be free, otherwise…

The governor had appointed a judge to hear the case as he had stated. However, Tonyn had left it up to the Army to provide a prosecutor and the Navy a defender. Lord Anthony had immediately picked Knight to act in Lancaster's defense. He of all the other officers was the only one who didn't know the midshipman or Lum so it was felt he would be more objective.

He had also been present for Sir Percival and the flag captain's court martial after the flagship had been sunk. Therefore he was familiar with the proceedings. A knock at the cabin door broke Knight's train of thought.

"First Lieutenant, suh," the marine sentry announced and stood aside to let Lieutenant Brooks enter.

"It's time captain. Your cox'n has your gig ready."

"Thank you," Knight said as he buttoned his shirt, put on his coat and took a quick look at shoes. "Well, Mr. Brooks, *Neptune* is yours till I return."

"Aye, captain, I'll keep a sharp lookout." Brooks also knew about Knight having to fight a one-sided battle in a sinking ship right here at this anchorage.

I'll not let the damn rogues get within cannon range without being sighted, Brooks thought. *Nay, the buggers will find a heated welcome should they try it again.*

"Gentlemen, this trial is called to order," the judge called from his seat behind a large table. "While we have military officers in key roles please remember this is a civil matter and as the defendant has waived his right to a jury, I will decide as to the verdict, innocent or guilty. Is there any questions?"

Since neither the Army provost, a Major Macpherson, nor Captain Knight had any questions, the judge continued.

"As long as order is maintained I will allow those interested into the courtroom. I will allow each of you a quarter hour then we will start. Major Macpherson, you will begin."

Lord Anthony and Gabe sat behind Knight and Midshipman Lancaster and listened as Macpherson went through the incident with the soldier who was a Corporal Johnson.

"Now Johnson," Macpherson's thick brogue resonated throughout the courtroom, "On the night in question did you provoke the midshipman before he attempted to murder…ere before he assaulted you?"

"No suh," the corporal sounded off as if he was on parade.

"Did you slander the midshipman in any way?"

"No suh."

Unable to contain himself, Gabe whispered to Lord Anthony, "A shilling says the lout doesn't even know what the word slander means."

"We have all been made aware of your grievous injuries so we will not go into specifics, but tell me now corporal, were you intoxicated to the point you may have said or did something that was so objectionable to cause Mr. Lancaster to act so violently?"

"No suh."

"Very well," Macpherson said and turned to Knight and made a slight bow.

Knight approached the corporal and said, "Tell me, do you know what it means to tell the truth?"

"No suh," the corporal responded automatically as he'd been doing then realized what he'd said. He tried to correct himself but before he could the courtroom erupted in laughter.

"Could you define intoxicated, corporal?" Knight asked as soon as things were quieted.

"Sir," Macpherson said rising, and then looking at the judge he said, "We are not here to discuss this man's vocabulary."

Knight then turned to the corporal and said, "Do you drink?"

"Yes suh!"

"Have you ever been drunk?"

"Yes suh!"

"When you get drunk do you often pick fights?"

"No suh!"

The corporal continued to answer but started to sweat as the last few pointed questions were asked.

Seeing Johnson sweat, Knight continued, "Do you ever get drunk and desire men?"

"No suh! I ain't no sodimite suh."

"But you do like to bully young boys don't you corporal?"

"No suh!"

Looking at the pitiful man Knight figured he'd never get more out of him. "No more questions," he said.

Major Macpherson then stood, "I have nothing further. I feel it is evident the accused acted impulsively over some imagined slight or insult and should be punished for his actions."

"Indeed?" the judge replied. "Captain Knight, do you have a witness for the defense?"

"Yes sir, I do." Then making a quick decision he continued, "I have two witnesses but I feel one could add very little other than to attest to the corporal's character and I feel we are all aware of that at this point."

This comment caused Macpherson to raise his eyebrows but he didn't respond. Knight then called Lum. After Lum was sworn in, Knight asked several questions to establish Lum's presence and his witnessing the event.

"Now, Lum, the defendant states he was accosted by the corporal. Is that what you saw?"

"Well suh, I don't rightly know what dat word accosted means but I see'd dat sodjer grab Mistah Lancaster's arse and try to kiss 'em. Ata' Mr. Lawrence slapped 'em a wallop, dat sodjer says he's gona make poh Mistah Lancaster squeal lak a pig. He den started biten on Mistah Lancaster's ear and bit it clean off. Then Mistah Lancaster shot 'em wid a pistol."

"Thank you, Lum," Knight said, amazed at how the black man had told his story without being prompted, unlike the corporal. Then not to be outdone, Knight turned to Macpherson and gave an exaggerated bow.

Macpherson seemed to be thinking, then approached Lum and said in an audible whisper, "Would you lie for the midshipman?"

"Lawd Gawd, no," Lum cried out, "Not ata' I done sworn to tells the truth. Maybe if I hadn't sworn on dat bible I mightun' stretch thangs a mite but Lum don't lie oncst he done laid his hand on God's word."

The judge tried not to smile at Lum's frank honesty.

"Well," Macpherson continued, "Lum, you said you were at a table sitting by the stairs?"

"Yah suh!"

"And you said the corporal and Lancaster was standing about five feet away with Lancaster facing the bar and Johnson facing toward the fireplace?"

"Yah suh! Dats de way it was."

"And you saw Johnson bite off Lancaster's ear?"

"Yah suh!"

"Humph! Tell me Lum," Macpherson said picking up the bible from the judge's table, "Can you see my hand through this bible?"

"No suh. I shore can't."

"Then tell me," Macpherson said sarcastically, "How you saw through Mr. Lancaster's head to see Johnson biting off his ear? Now the truth is sir, you didn't really see Johnson biting off the ear did you?"

"Naw," Lum said with his eyes looking upwards seemingly in deep thought. "Nah suh, thinking back I don't recon I can truthfully sat I saw dat sodjer bittin' off Mr. Lancaster's eah."

Damn, thought Knight.

However after a slight pause Lum continued his testimony, "But he was looking straight at me when he spat it out."

Upon hearing Lum's statement the courtroom erupted into hysterical laughter. It was several minutes before order could be restored.

Chapter Eleven

The day had dawned clear and warm with a humid sea breeze blowing its way across the harbour and onto the land around Saint Augustine.

Sir Raymond Knight had not slept well. After the trial, which ended in complete dismissal of all charges against Lancaster, he had gone along with Gabe, Markham and Stephen Earl to have a "victory wet" at the Mermaid. That is when he saw her. Domingo Chavez had a daughter, a goddess. Knight was immediately struck by the woman's beauty.

Her hair fell in ringlets and was black as a raven's wings, her eyes as green as the emerald sea; and her lips…lips as red as a ruby. She was medium height, slender and moved with a graceful light step. She had looked into Knight's eyes and he felt as if he'd always known this lovely creature he'd just met. He knew instantly however that she was the one he wanted to spend the rest of his life with.

Gabe had been talking about the sudden uproar of laughter during the trial when Lum had said matter-of-factly, "but I seen him when he spat it out."

Glancing Knight's way, then following his gaze to the beautiful Spanish girl it was all to clear to Gabe what held Knight's attention. He felt a pang of jealously as he thought of Faith in Savannah, not a day's sail away.

However, being the good shipmate he was, Gabe declared to all at the table, "Damme, but I do believe Sir Raymond has been struck by one of cupid's arrows." Pointing out the beauty that had captured Knight's eye, Markham and Earl had joined in on the tirade, "Damned if he ain't." The results of which cost him a round to shut everybody up.

Now glancing at his watch, Knight found it was time to report to the flagship for a meeting. Well he'd go to the meeting and if duty allowed he'd stop by the Mermaid and maybe meet up with this dark-skinned woman who had already captured his heart. Nancy…damned if the name wasn't lovely too.

By the time Lord Anthony's captains had gathered in his dining area the sea breeze had died but the heat and humidity remained ever present.

The attitude of Captain Buck when he entered the dining area seemed to be as oppressive as the heat and humidity. Today there would be no jokes or toasts. Today was business.

When Lord Anthony entered with Bart at his side everyone sat anxiously awaiting…news, new orders or whatever his lordship had on his mind.

"Gentlemen," Lord Anthony started off, "we are doing little to achieve our mission with our current plan so therefore we are going to make some changes. First, we are going after information. Something we have very little of. I want every ship, island trader or bumboat you encounter on your patrols stopped, searched and questioned."

While no one spoke, all knew for his lordship to be taking such aggressive action the Governor must be applying pressure. However, other than the action in which *Neptune* had been captured, all had been relatively quiet. *Swan* had captured a small island schooner that held a party of rebels raiding coastal villages.

Noting the look of dismay on his officers' faces Lord Anthony continued on, "These are trying times gentlemen and desperate measures are called for. You will be given your sailing orders before you leave. Now is there or has there been anything unusual within the city or the harbour that you've recognized?"

Gabe started to speak but held his tongue. Dagan had told him of a conversation with Bart while having a wet and enjoying a bowl of tobacco. A jollyboat had passed close to *Warrior's* stern. The passengers in the boat were mostly drunk and speaking very loudly. Bart had turned to Dagan and said, "Damned Dagos, everywhere you turn they's one and now we's can't even have a quiet evening without their blabbering spoiling it."

After hearing Dagan out Gabe went topside to view the harbour and verify Dagan's concerns.

When no one spoke up Lord Anthony said, "We'll leave it to two old tarpaulins to see and hear the obvious. Not to make a scene gentlemen but on your way back to your ships take note of how many Spanish vessels are at anchor here or inside the harbour. Listen to the talk in boats plying back and forth. It's mostly Spanish. When we are in port our ships are being attacked, when we're out they're not. The Governor was undoubtedly right about spies in the Spaniard's quarters."

"But Lord Anthony," Lieutenant Kerry from the *Pigeon* had stood, "we are not at war with Spain and Saint Augustine used to belong to Spain so how do we get rid of the Spanish without creating a national incident and maybe even bring them into war with the Colonies?"

"Well sir," Anthony answered the young lieutenant, "nobody said anything about getting rid of the Spanish. What I said was gather information. If that brings us to open conflict so be it. Most feel it will only be a matter of time and both the French and the Spanish will enter the war with the Colonials. I'm almost certain the French will."

"Now before you go, Captain Buck will give each of you your orders. Thanks to Captain Markham who recently captured the little island schooner, *Rose*, we now have means of communication with the Governor. *Pigeon* and *Audacity* will now be used to communicate between the flagship and the patrols."

This brought smiles from the gathered officers who knew it was a compliment for the admiral to address a lieutenant as a captain even if he was commanding a ship.

Gabe, Markham, and Earl were saying their goodbyes to Bart when Knight approached in tow with Buck.

"Damme sir, but I do hope this war hasn't spoiled our fearless captain's romance," Markham chimed.

Seeing the mischief in Markham's eye, Buck asked, "Who pray tell has been smitten?"

In unison the group replied, "Sir Raymond."

"Humph!" Buck said with an exaggerated frown. "Well, maybe I should do the honorable thing and keep this maiden well entertained while our brave captain is away doing his duty. I'm sure it's a service Sir Raymond would perform for me if I was away on King's business."

This caused a round of applause and laughter by all but Knight who seeing his cox'n was ready said, "I shall depart to my ship but you gentlemen can go to hell."

This brought out an uproar again. Markham laughed till tears poured from his eyes. Buck then raised his hand to quiet the group then said, "Dry your tears Captain Markham. Then if you and Captain Anthony can make your way to his lordship's cabin without demeaning some poor soul along the way, make yourself available to your admiral."

Then turning to Captain Earl, Buck said, "Let's share a glass while his Lordship talks to our wayward lads, and then he will tell you about orders."

Looking out Buck could see Knight's gig approaching *Neptune*. "Tsk, tsk," he said, "had our Sir Raymond not been in such a hurry he could have enjoyed a glass with us. Now, however, he will have to gather the gig crew together and that time will be spent rowing back to the flagship."

Seeing the Fifth Lieutenant Johns, Buck ordered, "Please make to *Neptune*. Captain repair on board."

This brought a chuckle from Earl but he'd seen the black-haired beauty that infatuated Knight and damned if he wasn't a bit smitten himself.

Oh well, Knight will be good and thirsty by time he returns in this heat. *Do him good*, Earl thought, *I should have seen her first.*

Chapter Twelve

Lord Anthony's meeting with Gabe and Markham brought mixed feelings from Gabe. An attempt to occupy Savannah was to be undertaken sometime next year. However, to prevent such a fiasco as the attempt to occupy Charlestown, time would be first spent gathering intelligence as to resistance and help from Loyalists.

Since a group of Colonial militia had broken into the Powder Magazine in May of 1775, the area had been relatively quiet on behalf of the Colonials. In January 1776, British warships entered the Savannah River without resistance and on March 2 and 3 of that same year, British ships again entered the Savannah Harbour and seized several merchant vessels laden with rice.

Lord Anthony explained all this then said, "Thomas Browne was sorely treated in his own residence on the South Carolina side of the Savannah River. He has convinced the Governor that other than the little town of Thunderbolt, minimal resistance would be met were we to seize Savannah."

"Do you think his motivation is revenge for his treatment or do you think he is earnest in his feelings about minimal resistance from Loyalist?"

After a momentary pause, Lord Anthony said, "I'm sure it's both. He wanted to be part of the intelligence gathering but we thought this unwise as he's so well known. So he's sending one of his rangers who knows the area well. Gabe, you and Lum will also do some intelligence gathering. You will pose as a seafaring man which you should be able to pull off."

This brought a chuckle from Markham.

"However," Lord Anthony continued, "You will leave your uniform on board *SeaWolf.* I don't have to tell you what this means if you get caught. I thought you could take Lum with you and that will help your cover. You know the coast but I'm told there's a small island...Warsaw Island, where you, Lum and Browne's ranger, a man named Finch can be put ashore. You will rendezvous back there at such time as you set up. While you are attending to your assignment, your first lieutenant will sail in the company with Markham, up the coast and back keeping an eye open for the likely lair of our privateer men."

"Markham?"

"Aye, my Lord."

"If it appears safe you may take a peek into the Savannah River up to the harbour entrance and see what reaction you get."

"Aye, sir."

"Very well gentlemen, you may be on your way."

As the two rose to take their leave, Lord Anthony spoke again, almost an after thought. "Gabe, one moment please."

Once Markham was out of the cabin, Lord Anthony went from being the Admiral to the older brother. Placing his hand on Gabe's shoulder he said, "If duty allows I would not think it amiss if you were to visit a friend."

Gabe smiled and grasping his brother's hand said, "Thanks, Gil."

Under full sail, *SeaWolf* and *Swan* cut through the ocean waters like a hot knife through butter. Gunnells, the master, stood by the helm and spoke to Gabe who was perched by the taffrail.

"It'd make a purty painting sir. Two nimble ships built for speed and doing what they were meant for, slicing through the water like God's own cheeks blew the wind that filled our sails."

"Aye," Gabe answered. He knew from looking at *Swan* under full sail that an artist who could capture the appearance on canvas would indeed have a purty painting. "Too bad we can't build such ships."

The comparison of Colonial shipwrights with the British had long been a touchy subject with Gabe. The Colonial built ships tended to have taller, raked masts and a waist more slender. Graceful ships made for speed. He had once been called down by his brother, who was then Captain Anthony, about his remark, *"we build tubs while they build ships."*

"Deck there," the lookout called down, "Convoy! To the suth'erd, ten...no...twelve sail she be."

At this time, Jackson, the first lieutenant, made his way aft. "The convoy from Antigua?"

"Those are my thoughts," Gabe responded.

Dagan glanced at Gabe and instantly knew his thoughts were also on that convoy they had escorted through this area last year. The traitorous renegade captain on board one of the ships almost cost Gabe his life.

"Deck there," the lookout called again, "Signal close with convoy!"

Damme, Gabe thought, *it won't hurt to be sociable for a spell.* As *SeaWolf* and *Swan* closed with the convoy Dagan nudged Gabe and pointed out a ship.

"She's the *Wild Goose.* Wonder if Estes still commands her."

"I haven't been told otherwise," Gabe said, "Do you see the *Lancaste*r brig?"

"No, she's probably sunk by now," Dagan answered with a smile. The brig had been so "wormy" Gabe had been surprised she'd made the voyage the previous year.

"There's the charge ship," Jackson volunteered, pointing to a thirty-two gun frigate.

"She be the *Lowestoffe*," Gunnells interjected. "Captain William Locker, no less, knew 'em when 'e was a middy."

Lieutenant Horatio Nelson greeted Gabe and Markham at *Lowestoffe's* entry port. "My apologies for your being detained," Nelson said after his greeting. "We have been attacked by privateers and lost one of our escort ships. Captain Locker is fit to be tied. He's hoping for help escorting this convoy as we are now down to two escort ships."

After the brief greeting Nelson escorted the two down to Captain Locker's cabin. After a glass of claret and much bending over a chart of the Georgia and South Carolina coasts, Captain Locker thanked Gabe and Markham and voiced his appreciation of their willingness to sail along and help protect the convoy till they were off the North Carolina coast.

SeaWolf and *Swan* were sailing under private orders so he couldn't order them to help but it never hurt to lend a helping hand when it could be done within the discretion allowed by their orders. "You never know when you might need a hand," Gabe's father, Admiral James Anthony, had always stated.

Several days later *SeaWolf* and *Swan* were on a tack to put them off the Savannah coast at nightfall. Gabe, Gunnells, Jackson and the Ranger Finch were bending over the master charts in the captain's cabin.

"I ain't no sailor," Finch was saying. "But I've fished these waters enough to know we need to get off the ship here at Warsaw Island," he said, pointing at the island on the chart, "then we can row up through this here inlet."

"That's Warsaw alright," Gunnells volunteered.

"Yeah, well," Finch continued, "I know the deep water channels through the marsh so we can get right up to here by daybreak."

"That's Thunderbolt!" Gunnells injected, causing Finch to give the master an irritated glare.

Finch gave Gunnells a sarcastic look for his interruption. After a moment of silence Finch continued, "This is Wilmington Island. Once we get to this area we have to be very cautious."

"Sometimes they's ships anchored there. Privateers frequently unload their plunder here so it wouldn't surprise me to find the area crowded. Best you let me and yo man do the talking if we meet up with anyone," Finch said to Gabe.

A knock at the door and the marine announced, "Second lieutenant, zur!"

Lavery entered and reported, "We're off the coast of Savannah now, sir. You can already see lights from the town."

"Very well," Gabe replied, "I'll be on deck directly."

Then turning to the group of men before him he said, "Well, men, you know your duties so I'll not detain you from making your final preparations."

As the last man had filed out of the cabin Dawkins came out of the pantry with two glasses. He handed one to Gabe and the other one to Dagan then made his way out leaving the two alone.

"I should be going with you," Dagan spoke first. "It's my place."

"I wish you could," Gabe replied, "but I need you here and it would be more difficult if we get stopped. There's no way you'd pass for a Georgian."

"And you would," Dagan bounced back but smiled as he did so.

"I know I wouldn't," Gabe acknowledged, "but unless I see Faith, I intend to let Lum and Finch do my talking."

"A toast then," Dagan said, "to the lady that holds your heart...and your ruby."

Finch's pipe bowl glowed red as he sat in the bow of the small boat they had brought with them from Saint Augustine. It was about fourteen feet long and about four feet wide. There was a pole lying inside the boat that was almost as long as the boat.

The boat had a flat bottom that Gabe had initially been skeptical of, but once inside the channel Finch had them put down the oars and took up the pole. Surprisingly to Gabe, Lum was also quite adept at poling the boat along.

The night, which at first had seemed very still and almost silent, soon gave over to a whole orchestra of sounds as the boat glided along in the dark waters; the flapping of fish jumping in the water after a bug; the sound of big bullfrogs croaking, the chirping of thousands of crickets and the buzz of the thrice damned mosquitoes.

"Got a pipe?" Finch asked Gabe after he'd slapped at his face for the hundredth time or more trying to fend off the devilish pests.

"Yes."

"Then light it up, it'll at least keep the bugs from around your head."

"What about the glow, won't somebody spot it?" Gabe asked the question that had been bothering him seeing the glow from Finch's pipe.

"Folks won't pay near as much mind to a glowing pipe as they would some fool keeps slapping hisself."

Hearing this exchange caused Lum to take a deep breath. Finch was right, but British officers didn't take it kindly when they were spoken to in such a way. To prevent any friction between the two Lum spoke up.

"Ya see cap'n, folks be on des waters all time at night fishing, so it seem natural seeing a man wid 'is pipe stoked up to ward off dem skeeters an utter bugs an' such. Seeing us wid our pipes agoing ain't gonna rouse spicion in nobody. But a man dats slapping 'is face would be plum outta place."

Gabe realized the wisdom in Lum's words and stoked up his pipe. He was surprised at the immediate relief from the skeeters.

As the trio passed Wilmington Island there were three ships at anchor. One was larger and Gabe could sense she was a privateer. Well, maybe they had discovered one of the privateers' lairs.

After what seemed like an eternity Finch said, "This is it. That's Thunderbolt and it's only a few miles walk to Savannah. Now I know a man here who lives close to the water. We'll turn the boat over and leave it upside down at his place. Ya'll stay with the boat while I go up to his house. If it's all clear I'll hoot."

Not wanting to be thought the fool for anything else Gabe waited till Finch had gone up to the house before asking Lum, "What's a hoot?"

"Dat's da sound what an owl makes," Lum explained. "Some of dem fellers at Beaufort were right good at it. They'd wait till some girl's daddy was asleep then they'd go stand under da girl's bedroom window and hoot. Sometimes if he was lucky the girl would sneak outta the window and they'd go sashaying off for a spell."

Then a big smile crossed Lum's face making his teeth shine in the dark. "Course one time I's told this girl went to sleep waiting on a fellah and so he hooted and hooted to wake her up only he woke up her daddy, who poked de barrel of his gun outta da window and said, 'If dats an owl 'e sick and needs killin and iffen it ain't no owl it needs to be getting 'foh 'e 'as to go to picken lead outta 'is arse.'"

Lum's narration all but made Gabe forget where he was and when Finch's hoot finally came it made him jump.

Chapter Thirteen

It was early in the afternoon when Gabe and Lum made their way to the Lacy home. He'd gotten directions from Finch's friend who plainly was nervous at the thought of Gabe accompanying him and Finch on their mission, said, "Rest assured they'd be a threat to us if we was to meet up with any Colonials and they started to ask questions. I insist that we go alone and you," the man said emphasizing the word "you" to Finch, "Can meet up with them later after we've done our business." Therefore they set off in different directions.

As they got close to Savannah Lum's pace quickened, "I knows where we at now, suh, just you fallah me."

The lane was filled with crushed shells. Huge oak trees with hanging moss grew on either side of the lane that made a circle in front of the house. The house was a three-story affair flanked on each side with a two-story wing. There was a veranda that was adorned with four white fluted columns running the full length in front. The house was brick and the only oddity was it had blue shutters. On each end of the house a white wooden swing hung on chains.

As Gabe and Lum approached an elderly black man clad in a well-tailored black suit with a white shirt and a gray sash about his middle stepped out the huge ornate door.

It was obvious the servant recognized Lum, who called, "Howdy Henry, where is Nanny and Missy Faith?"

Hearing her name, Faith stepped out on the porch and felt her heart pound at the sight of the approaching men, "Gabe, oh my God, Gabe, it's you?"

Gabe's heart began to pound, his knees felt weak, he could barely breathe as he stood in awe at the sight of Faith. If anything she was more beautiful than he remembered. He raced up the steps to this woman who held his heart. Her blonde hair hung loose over her shoulder and he could feel its softness as their arms embraced one another.

Her smell, her softness, the pent-up passion as their lips met, both hungry with longing and desire. When finally they broke their kiss Faith was gasping, here was her man. Still embracing Gabe, Faith felt his body stiffen and try to take a step back but with her holding him so tight he was unable to do so. Then sensing someone else on the porch Faith turned and saw why Gabe had stiffened.

"Aunt Caroline...this if Gabe...he's...," Faith not sure if she should reveal Gabe's identity or not finally said, "he's my fiancé!"

"I see," Caroline replied, "but child if you don't let loose of him there will be no wedding. You've fairly squeezed the breath out of this young man." Then smiling Caroline reached out her hand to Gabe and said, "And a handsome young man he is too Faith, no wonder your so moonstruck. Seeing the two of you tangled up pure gave me the vapors. Now come in the house before we shock any passerby and they die of apoplexy."

At that time the rustle of feet could be heard and Nanny rushed in. One hand had Lum in tow while the other fanned her face. "Would you look a heah, child, what da debble done brung up and left at our doh steps. Fact is ole Nanny's heart is jus' a flip-flopping like some ole catfish what done been caught and drug up on da creek bank."

"Mine too, Nanny, mine too."

Gabe felt some flutters himself but was in strange territory and was at a loss for words.

Not so with Lum. He walked over to Faith who gave him a big hug, then Lum volunteered, "I been takin' care of de cap'n foh you missy, jus' lak I promised you I'd do. I been right by his side and we's been doing fine. 'Ceptin' I knows the cap'n been missin' you. Yes mam, he sho' nuff has. I see him holden on to dat little bag round his neck and starin' out into de ocean and I knows who he's thinking bout."

"Well, thank you Lum," Faith said using her dress sleeve to dry the tears that started with Lum's words.

Sensing the need to leave Faith and Gabe alone, Nanny said, "Well come on heah you ole rascal, I know you must be hungry."

As the two left for the kitchen Caroline said, "So you're a ship's captain, Gabe?"

Oh hell, Faith thought, *Lum let the cat out of the bag.*

Gabe, deciding not to lie, said, "Yes ma'am, although I don't look like it, I command a British ship of war." He then added a little lie, "I wanted to see Faith and knew I wouldn't be well received dressed in my uniform, therefore these clothes."

"You realize you could be shot as a spy?" This from a man who entered the foyer from what appeared to be an office or library.

Turning to the man, Gabe replied, "Matter of fact it was a risk I was willing to take in order to see Faith."

A silence filled the room and Gabe sized up the man standing before him. He was of medium height, short brown hair that was graying at the temples and balding on top, a man that would not wear one of those stylish wigs. He was barrel-chested and had a weather-beaten tanned face. He had deep-set green eyes and wore white pants and a dark blue frock coat.

Gabe knew the man's clothes were of the finest quality. He also knew by the way the man spoke and carried himself he had spent many a hour on a quarterdeck. The sailor in him was unmistakable. This had to be Faith's dead father's partner, Gavin Lacy.

Lacy held Gabe's gaze for another moment then broke the silence. "Well said young sir. I like it when a man knows what he wants and is willing to risk all for it."

During the exchange Faith had sided up to Gabe and again put her arm around him.

"I'm pleased to meet you," Lacy continued and held out his hand, "For now I welcome you as a guest. We'll talk about other matters later."

Gabe breathed a sigh of relief and relaxed.

Later that night after gorging himself on a fine southern supper, Gabe sat in the swing with Faith in his arms.

"How long can you stay?" she asked.

"I leave at daybreak."

"Take me with you."

Gabe's heart almost stopped. "I can't," he finally replied, "I've no place for you right now. A ship is not place for a woman…and…Faith you once said you couldn't marry me as our countries were at war. Does that still hold true?"

"Oh no, Gabe, I'm so sorry I said that. You don't know how many times I wish I could have taken those words back."

At that time Gabe could see Lacy rounding the porch on the far side of the house. He was holding a long-stemmed corncob pipe and was lighting it. It was similar to the one Lum smoked but the "bowl" was over three inches high.

Seeing Lacy, Gabe stood from the swing, "Mr. Lacy, may I have a word with you, sir?"

Lacy made his way over to the far end of the porch where the two young lovers were then sat down in a white rocking chair that was beside the swing. Gabe sat back down by Faith who nestled up close to him.

Mr. Lacy," Gabe began, "I love Faith and desire to make her my wife. I've put enough prize money up that I can care for her in a manner of which she is accustomed. I would like your blessing on this union."

Seeing Faith's face light up, Lacy said, "You have it of course." Then he noted Gabe had raised his hand to interrupt him.

"However, you know sir that I'm a British officer, what you don't know and neither does Faith, but I think its important you know now before you give your blessing, is my father, who was an admiral, and my mother, who was a gypsy, lived together for over twenty years. They were never married, sir." Then taking a deep breath and exhaling slowly Gabe continued, "I'm a bastard."

"Hmmph!" Lacy snorted. "Aren't we all at some time or another? That changes nothing. You have my blessings, sir, regardless."

"Oh, Uncle Gavin," Faith leapt from the swing making the chains creak and groan.

Gabe stood and shook Lacy's hand, "Thank you sir."

"Think nothing of it young man. Now just between the two…uh, three of us, should I expect to see warships in the harbour?"

Gabe fell silent for a moment then said, "Just between the three of us I wouldn't worry this year. However, I'd not speak of anytime after that."

"I see," Lacy said as he rose. "Rest assured this conversation will go no further. Now, I'll let the two of you alone as you only have but another quarter hour before Faith has to retire."

Chapter Fourteen

A fog drifted over the lowlands. The distinct smell of the marsh was very evident on the gentle sea breeze. The tide was coming in. It was a tearful departure. Faith's goodbye kiss was hot and passionate and salty as the tears flowed from her face.

"I will see you as soon as I can," Gabe promised. He had offered to let Lum stay behind but Lum would hear nothing of it.

"We'll come back time to time and when dis heah wars over we'll come back to stay."

Making their way back to the rendezvous, Gabe said, "I just don't know, Lum. This whole situation makes no sense."

Lum could feel the melancholy Gabe was experiencing. He paused and laid his hand on Gabe's shoulder then said, "Yo problem cap'n is you don't hate dem whats we's fighting against and you don't love what we's fighting for. I don't reckon you's even knows dis King what making the war. But foh me, you's give me freedom. So's I'm yo' cabin servant, I'm paid to do it and iffen I was to decide to quit, I could. Iffen I'd stayed behind I'd jus been a slave."

Well, I'm not much more, Gabe thought, but understood the wisdom in the old black man's words.

Finch was waiting as had been planned. Gabe could see the man was nervous and fidgety.

"We've got to take a detour on the way back. Seems a frigate has tied up at Wilmington Island. I don't want to chance getting stopped by coming too close. I know another way. A little rougher and longer but it'll bypass the island."

"But I want to see this ship," Gabe insisted, "even if we have to wait until dark." He could sense Finch's anger but the ranger held it in check.

"You hankering to get shot up or have your neck stretched? That's what they'll do or worse if we're caught. You ever see'd a man skint?"

"I trust your abilities, Mr. Finch. If we need to take to the marsh after I've seen the ship so be it, but I'm going to take a look."

Sighing Finch relented saying, "It's your funeral."

Gabe was not happy with Finch's idea of getting past the privateer but he didn't have a better one. An old canvas was "borrowed" from someone's fishing boat. It was under this canvas Gabe hid. A hole was cut in it so he'd have a good view. The heat from being under the canvas was bad enough but the stench from the "ripe" old cloth was made worse when Finch raided some poor souls trout line and piled the fish on top of the canvas. It added to the disguise but Gabe swore to himself he'd never eat another fish.

Finch sat in the bow of the boat with a fishing pole while Lum in the stern poled them past the ship and Wilmington Island. When given the all clear to get out from beneath the canvas Gabe was soaking wet with sweat.

"Stay low," Finch warned, "In case you have to duck beneath that canvas again sudden like."

Gabe took a long swig of warmish water. He rinsed his mouth with the water, spit over the side then took a drink. "She was a frigate alright but not the *Barracuda*. She was the *Edisto*."

"More-'n-likely," Finch drawled, "she's owned by someone close by being named Edisto. There are two rivers and a town with the same name."

Made sense, Gabe thought.

"She had fourteen gun ports this side," Finch said. "That'd make her a twenty-eight?"

"Well, she probably carries two chase guns forward and two aft," Gabe answered, "so I'd bet she's a thirty-two at least and looks French built."

"Well, they're talking about her in Thunderbolt like she's something special," Finch said. "Man said she'd taken twenty prizes full of trade goods and military supplies."

Gabe had noticed the use of "man" said and not a name mentioned. Whatever else Finch was, he was careful not to reveal a source. He'd already told Gabe not to count on help from loyalists in Thunderbolt. Unlike Savannah, where there were large numbers of people who were against the war, the folks in Thunderbolt were very much in favor of the revolution.

Well good news or bad, Gabe thought, *they'd succeeded in their initial fact finding mission.* He smiled to himself; maybe his personal mission was a little more successful. He now knew his love for Faith was not one-sided. The only thing that would keep the two of them apart would be death. Well, that was a real possibility with this damn war.

Lum broke Gabe's reverie when he said, "We's heah and I believe dem's sails out dar on da horizon."

"Aye," Gabe replied, "Two sets of sails. Let's just hope they're ours and not some damn privateer trying to make it back to his lair."

Chapter Fifteen

A cutting out…Gabe…we are supposed to be on a fact finding mission and return with our facts," Markham exclaimed as he paced about in his cabin.

The *Swan* and *SeaWolf* had made the rendezvous as planned. Sitting at the mouth of the inlet and waiting to be picked up, Gabe had formed a plan to cut out if possible, and if not possible to cut out, then burn the *Edisto*. Once out of sight of land, Gabe had signaled *Swan* to heave to.

Though senior to Markham, Gabe had himself rowed over to the *Swan* to present his plan. He would need some of Markham's men to carry out the plan. Now as always Markham was in a tirade at the mention of such a daring plan.

"Gabe, have you forgotten what happened last time?" Markham saw the hurt look on Gabe's face but he continued, "Facts, Gabe, not heroics. Has something addled your brain?" Markham continued on, "You know damn well what our orders say."

"Aye!" Gabe answered his friend, "But Francis, sometimes we have to take initiative."

Upon hearing Gabe use his first name Markham rolled his eyes.

"Besides," Gabe continued, "you can take Finch and head on back to Saint Augustine. All I want is your marines and Mr. Davy."

"Humph! It's not enough to lose your midshipman over some damn foolish incident, you can't wait to chance mine."

After Lancaster's trial, he had been transferred to another ship. Although they had won the trial, they felt that to stay in Saint Augustine would be a constant reminder and irritation to the garrison soldiers. So, Lord Anthony transferred Lancaster, and as of yet Gabe had not gotten a replacement.

Shaking his head and giving a sigh Markham agreed. "But damme, Gabe, if you come out of this alive you owe me. Not just a round. Nay, you owe me a whole evening and maybe a little sporting to boot."

"You got it," Gabe exclaimed pounding his friend on the back. "I'll send Finch over and you can transfer Davy and the marines. We'll leave at dusk so we can be back at first light or sooner. *Swan* and *SeaWolf* can stand offshore and watch for a flare. That's the signal to pick us up."

"And if there's no flare by sunrise?" Markham asked.

Solemnly Gabe replied, "Then it's up to you as I doubt we'll be back."

The sky had darkened and stars began to twinkle and take shape. The weather held with a wind blowing briskly on the larboard beam. *This should help the rowers*, Gunnells thought as he put *SeaWolf* in position to offload the cutting out party.

Gabe was in cabin with Dagan, Lavery, Davy and Marine Lieutenant Baugen. Jackson was there also but more to listen than anything else. He'd already made his argument why he and not Gabe should be leading the expedition. Gabe tried to salve his feelings by explaining he knew the layout and that would make things much easier.

"Besides," Gabe explained, "I have to have someone I trust in command of *SeaWolf* in my absence."

As the group listened intently Gabe explained, "We are still out of sight of land but I've ordered Gunnells to plot us a course so we'll stand in about here," pointing to a spot on the chart spread across his table. "We should make our way inland in the boats just at nightfall. I want Mr. Davy's launch to attack on the starboard quarter. Have your axe men ready, Mr. Davy. As soon as convenient have them cut the cables both forward and aft. This should set the ship adrift and with the current float her down river. Hopefully we'll have enough speed for steerage."

"Mr. Lavery, you will take the men in your launch on the starboard quarter and board. Taking control of the quarterdeck is your main objective."

"Dagan, you will be in charge of the launch with the marines and board from the larboard side. I will take the gig and board larboard side also. We will attack aft and help secure the quarterdeck while you and the marines board forward. Hopefully, we will have a foothold when your group boards at the main chains. Send some of the marines to the main riggings. They are to ignore whatever fighting is going on, on deck. I want them in place to mark down anyone or group that maybe making a stand."

"Mr. Lavery, once the quarterdeck is taken I want you to send men to loosen the main topsail and sheet it home. If I'm killed or wounded, Mr. Lavery will take command. Is there any question?"

When no one spoke up, Gabe said, "Very well, I'll let you go tend to last minute details. But remember we need the element of surprise so make sure no musket or pistol is cocked. All it would take is for some clumsy idiot to drop a weapon and it go off to ruin all we've worked to accomplish. And possibly make us guests to the rebels." This brought a chuckle from the gathered men.

The boat crews had manned the boats and they had been paid off. Gabe went down into the gig as it heaved on the dark water. He gave the command to shove off in a voice barely above a whisper. Gabe took the tiller as he sat in the stern sheets. As the men pulled slowly Gabe looked back just in time to see *SeaWolf* disappear in the night. *Would she be there to pick them up at dawn as planned… Would they be there as planned? Faith, if he were killed what would she do? Would she mourn?*…All kinds of nagging doubts seemed to rush through Gabe's head.

Silently the boats made their way into the inlet and up the rivers. Time seemed to crawl. The night was unusually quiet; no croaking bullfrogs, no chirping crickets, no fish jumping. An occasional buzz of a mosquito was the only thing to break the sound. Muffled oars continued to row for what seemed like an eternity then they were there. The frigate was there in the shadows. A couple of lanterns burned dimly but Gabe could see no movement on board the vessel.

"Heave ho!" Gabe ordered in a whisper.

As the boats came together the frigate was visible to all as she rode at her moorings, her mast and spars just visible, almost like shadows in a nighttime sky.

"Everyone ready?" Gabe inquired.

"Good, then let's be about our business. Give way," Gabe ordered, as the boats made their way to the sleepy unsuspecting frigate.

The privateer's crew had spent many nights tied up here off Wilmington Island. The standard precautions against night attack had fallen to haphazard routine as everyone felt safe in the shielded anchorage. There was no reason for tonight to be any different than the night before or the night before that.

As Gabe's boats drew abeam of the frigate the sound of a woman's laughter could be heard below decks, then a drunken shout to clam up or go over the side. A giggle was the response. The boats were now in position and quietly the seamen and marines boarded at their assigned positions. As luck would have it just as the last marine was on board a woman needing to relieve herself, made her way topside. Seeing a strange man she let out a scream. Without realizing he was facing a woman the marine smashed the woman in the face with the butt of his musket, felling her like a downed oxen.

However, the sound caused the lone sentry to emerge with a lantern. Seeing the deck filling with boarders he fired his musket at a nearby figure. The flash of the musket lit up a wave of boarders. Unfortunately, it was the last thing the sentry saw as a sailor crushed his skull with a boarding pike. The rush of feet could be heard as men and women alike poured out of the hatchways.

Gabe found himself being attacked by two people; one was a mulatto woman who must have been the wife of the man attacking him with a cutlass. Suddenly in desperation, as Gabe was winning the battle with the man, the woman bare-handedly grabbed Gabe's sword. Without thinking he snatched the weapon back slicing open the woman's fingers, severing tendons and arteries. The sight of his deed caused Gabe to become sickened as the woman fell to the deck screaming, trying to staunch the blood flow with useless hands.

Seeing his wife's ruined hands, the enraged husband began his attack anew, only to be shot through the center of his chest. Glancing to his left Gabe could see Lum with the still smoking pistol in his hands and just behind him Dagan. The fighting was once again thrust their way pushing Gabe back to the larboard bulwark. There were screams and shouts followed by cries of agony as men fought hand to hand.

Dagan found himself entangled as someone who had fallen grabbed at his feet. Dagan kicked out with his feet to free himself from the hands that held him. Not being able to loosen himself from the man's death grip Dagan pulled his cutlass from his belt and thrust it downward stabbing the frantic privateer in the neck. Hot blood spewed out of the man's severed jugular and the deck became even more slippery.

Lavery's group fought and struggled with a savage group of privateers who had backed the British boarding party to the companion ladder. The marine marksmen made their presence known as one after another of the desperate privateers were marked down.

Gabe, Dagan and Lum continued to thrust and parry, stepping over dead and downed men. Forward there was more fighting going on. Both groups were yelling and cursing as the two groups emerged into one melee. Gabe felt a heavy blow as a crazed man attacked with a belaying pin. However, Gabe was now inflamed with a fighting madness. He struck down the man with his blade with such vehemence he severed the man's arm at the elbow. Seeing his arm hit the deck still holding the belaying pin the man ran and jumped over the railing into the black waters of the river.

Lum was now facing two attackers and felt a searing pain in his left shoulder. A third man had joined the melee. Dagan seeing the attack unfold had just reloaded his pistol and at point blank range fired, turning one of Lum's attacker's face into a bloody pulp. As the fight continued, Davy found himself next to Dagan and Lum. A huge man attacked Davy. The man's breath reeked of the rum that only minutes ago he'd been drinking. Drunkenly, the man lunged. Parrying the man's cutlass with his sword then stabbing up and inward with his dirk Davy punctured both the heart and lung. As he pulled his blade from between his foe's ribs a great sucking noise was made. The man's eyes suddenly went blank as he fell to his knees then face forward onto the deck.

There was a rush of feet as the British group rallied around Gabe. The few privateers left standing put down their weapons, all except one.

"Surrender sir," Gabe asked.

"I'll see you damned first," the man replied still in a rage. This had to be the captain and Gabe understood the man facing the reality of his magnificent ship falling into the enemy's hands. *Not like the feelings of the reported twenty prizes he'd taken*, Gabe surmised.

"Your sword sir," Gabe asked once again but the man was blind with fury. He sprang forward with a wild animal like cry oblivious to all but repelling these boarders who were taking his ship. As he lunged forward he found himself impaled with two bayonets as the marines had stepped forward to protect their captain.

Looking in disbelief at the bayonets in his chest the man's eyes glazed over and his sword clanged to the deck as his lifeless hand had let loose of the blade.

The madness in Gabe was now on the ebb. The ship was now clear except for the wounded and dead which lay about the deck. British sailors and marines limped around going about their duties as had been assigned.

It was then Dagan approached and said, "Someone cut the steerage cable so we have no rudder. We're drifting downstream but it won't be long I'm thinking before we'll be grounded."

"Very well," Gabe replied then called to Davy, "see to the boats. I don't want them swamped."

"Mr. Lavery?"

"Aye, cap'n."

"Get all the wounded together. We can put the privateer's men ashore. They can take their wounded with them."

"Lum?"

"Yes suh."

"Go gather up all the rags and things you can find and meet me at the magazine. Dagan, let's go check out the captain's cabin."

A through search of the captain's quarters turned up very little. A very nice set of dueling pistols in a box was tucked under Dagan's arm when they went topside. As they reached the main deck the ship gave a shudder, then a loud creaking of the timbers as the frigate grounded itself in a nearby mud bank. While the wounded men were being off-loaded Lum found a bale of rags and two barrels of coal oil. A barrel of linseed was also found. The rags were soaked in the coal oil then the ship was doused with the remainder. The linseed oil was in a huge barrel so Lum smashed the barrel with an axe sending the liquid gushing over the deck and down into the bowels of the ship.

A search of the magazine proved to be disappointing. Only two barrels of gunpowder was found.

"They were probably waiting on supplies," Dagan commented seeing the lack of powder.

"Well, we can use it to start the fire," Gabe said.

Back on the main deck everyone had been off-loaded. Lavery and Davy had everything ready for departure. The gunpowder was strewn across the deck and a line was poured to the entry port. Dagan threw the powder barrel he had been using to create a fuse back to the center of the deck then used his pistol to ignite the powder. The men had barely cleared the ship when the dark sky lit up like an inferno. The men were pulling with all their might but the heat from the ship could be felt by the men in the boats, making them pull with an urgency.

"That'll bring out a crowd I'm thinking," Dagan said as they rowed toward the inlet.

Looking back a red glow was visible with sparks and embers filling the sky like fireworks.

"She'd made a fine prize," Gabe said, regret at having to burn the ship in his voice.

"Aye, my thoughts as well," Dagan replied. "What a waste," he continued, "but she'll never take another British ship."

Chapter Sixteen

The trip back to Saint Augustine was very uneventful. The sky was clear, the wind steady. Dagan had challenged Caleb to a game of chess. Gabe watched intently but the game didn't engross him like it did Caleb and Dagan.

Lum, to get away from Mr. Jewels, took his lotz and went forward. Soon all the men not on watch had gathered round, most with their rum rations in their hands. Some downed their ration while others sipped at the metal cups, trying to make it last. A number of the men chewed tobacco, while most who smoked, lit up their pipes. A few had cigars and these were lit.

The crew was content after a successful operation, which yielded only a handful of wounded and no deaths. Down in the wardroom the master had Jackson in stitches with his bawdy humor. The purser who never smiled was even laughing at Gunnels's last rhyme, having to do with a hermit who had a dead wench in a cave.

Dawkins could hear the laughter from the wardroom as he passed it going back to the captain's cabin. He had put a bottle of hock in the bilges to chill and had gone to retrieve it now that it was cool enough to drink. It amazed him how cool things stayed below the waterline when the water itself felt warm to the touch. As he made his way into the cabin he could see Caleb leaning forward over the chess board frowning while Dagan was reared back with a smile across his face.

"Damme, sir, where in God's creation did you learn that move? I've not surrendered yet mind you, but it looks like its checkmate."

Caleb had got to where he spent a lot of time with Dagan. This had started after the overland trip to rescue Gabe, after stopping by Dagan's uncle's place seeking help for Gabe's rescue. He rarely spent much time away from his old traveling companion…was it a bond created by the trip or from a bond with Kitty, the uncle's daughter?

"I surrender," Caleb finally said.

Dawkins had gotten three glasses and was pouring the hock for the group. "This is the last bottle of hock, cap'n."

"Well, you'd better pour yourself a glass and enjoy what we have left," Gabe told his secretary.

This brought a smile to Dawkin's lips. "Don't worry, sir, it'll not go to waste."

"Likely he's been taking lessons from Bart," Dagan said.

"Well now Bart has learned a trick or two along the way," Dawkins answered, "But I believe I've got more time on the head than he's got in His Majesty's Navy."

This brought a chuckle from the group. Dawkins picked up the bottle with the remaining hock and ambled off toward the pantry.

As the ole man entered the pantry he heard Caleb asked, "Dagan, have you heard from your folks in Virginia lately?"

Gabe instantly picked up on Caleb's question and he eyed Dagan who was eyeing Caleb.

"You interested in the whole clan or was there somebody particular?" Dagan asked, his head tilted back and angled a bit, his arms across his chest.

"Well, I'd like to know about the whole family," Caleb stammered, "but I was...ah...I am particularly interested in how Kitty is doing."

Enjoying the riposte between his two friends Gabe couldn't help but feel sympathetic towards Caleb. He knew how he longed for Faith and even though it had been only a day or so he had a burning desire to be back with her, *to hold her, to feel those lips against his, to...ah...well...just to be with her*. Dagan clearing his throat broke Gabe's train of thought.

"Well there was a letter sometime back," Dagan said then left the sentence hanging.

"Well," Caleb prompted.

"Well, I think you need to study your chess game a little more," Dagan said as he continued to toy with Caleb.

"Damn the chess game man, the letter, was there anything in the letter about me?"

"Humph! Not that I recall."

Then seeing the forlorn look creep across Caleb's face, Dagan appeared to be deep in thought then said, "Well, maybe there was one bit where Uncle Andre said Kitty asked to be remembered to you and should you desire to come visit again you'd be welcome."

The joy that filled Caleb's face was unmistakable, then a frown, "Why, dammit all, Dagan, why didn't you tell me?" Caleb exclaimed in a perturbed manner.

"Cause you didn't ask," Dagan flung back.

"Humph!" Caleb then reached for his glass and downed the hock. "I think I'll go topside and listen to Lum before I retire. He at least knows something about manners."

As Caleb left the cabin Dagan looked at Gabe and smiled, "I expect we might be losing Caleb before too long."

"My thoughts as well," Gabe replied then noticed Dagan staring out the stern window into the dark.

"Not before he's needed though, not before he's needed." Dagan's quiet predictions always gave Gabe an eerie feeling. He watched in silence as without another word Dagan stood up from the table, reached for his pipe and tobacco then made his way out.

Not the way I would like for the evening to end, Dawkins thought as he sat in the pantry nursing the remains of the hock, *not the way I wanted it to end at all.*

By midday an easterly wind was blowing more than a half gale. On shore, Admiral Lord Anthony paused before he entered the governor's coach taking him back to Saint Augustine Harbour, where he would board his barge and make the trip out to the anchorage.

Unlike Antigua, Saint Augustine's channel entrance was too shallow to allow a ship of the line to enter the safety of the harbour. The ride from the governor's house was not a pleasant ride. Between potholes and the wind the coach rocked viciously. Looking out at the harbour Anthony could see the wind had churned the normally clear waters to a dark, cloudy appearance with the waves rushing ashore leaving all manner of crushed shells, jellyfish and other creatures in the sand.

It was coming on to hurricane season. That was the topic of the conversation with Governor Tonyn. Without a safe harbour, his ships, with the exception of *Audacity* and *Pigeon* who could enter the harbour, would have to stand off and possibly run before the wind. The governor, a landsman, admitted he'd never considered the safety of ships from the elements when he requested a naval presence. The meeting had hit a sour note but then Anthony reminded the governor any storm that created peril for his ships would do the same for privateers. This seemed to pacify Tonyn. The slamming of a shutter as the wind picked up, bending the palms outside Tonyn's office window added finality to the situation. A driving rain had started by the time Anthony made it to the harbour and his waiting barge.

He was tempted to have the coach take him back to the governor's house until the weather moderated but knew in the long run he'd be more comfortable aboard *Warrior* and away from politicians. Stepping down from the coach Anthony turned a shoulder to the wind and rain. He cocked his head to one side but still had to use his hand to keep his hat from blowing off his head. Out of nowhere Bart seemed to materialize with Dagan at his side. The two had likely made a trip to the Mermaid while he had been at the governor's. It was just as likely they had brought a bottle back to be shared by the barges crew.

As Anthony settled in the barge Bart handed him a boat cloak then adjusted his old tarpaulin.

"Winds sharper than a whore's tongue," Bart said to Anthony. Then turning his attention to the barge's crew ordered, "Stir your stumps mates; unlimber your timbers and pull."

The dripping sailors went about Bart's bidding confident a "tot" of rum waited them at the flagship. The bowman pushed off and the two banks of oars came down in perfect unison. Seemingly oblivious to the wind and rain, Anthony's mind was on the report Gabe and Markham had delivered upon their return the previous day.

They would have to spend more time patrolling that area for privateers. This was now obvious and it pleased Tonyn to hear they'd destroyed the privateer. Finch's report had also sounded promising. However, the more he thought about it Anthony was sure Bart had been right. The Spaniards were involved, but who and how? Too many questions and not enough answers.

Well, I'll keep the Carolina coast guessing as to when we might make an appearance, Anthony decided, *but I am going to focus on the south…the Keys and Havana.*

It was what Lord Anthony missed most of all when at sea. With nothing but open sky on the horizon and the deck lively beneath his feet, he would stand at the weather side of the quarterdeck and enjoy the peace of the early morn. Now Captain Earl leaned on the weather rail, as was his place. *Merlin* was his ship. Anthony had already deprived the captain of his quarters by shifting his flag to the *Merlin*. The loss of a cabin compared to the honour of flying the admiral's flag was an inconvenience most captains would gladly endure. Earl was no different.

Anthony had felt the desire…nay, the need to go on this patrol. He needed the feel of the sea vibrating through his body. He felt that if he could get back to the open sea he could get his mind in tune with the mission. He felt dry-docked at the Saint Augustine anchorage so he had shifted his flag to *Merlin* in spite of Captain Buck's protest.

Now they were almost to the Florida Keys. *SeaWolf* was in sight ahead and *Audacity* was off the weather side almost a beam. The sun was an hour above the horizon and already bearing down like a torch. The sky was a light blue and the sea a deep aqua. Under full sail *Merlin* ploughed her way through the rolling sea.

Bart approached with a mug in his hand. "A bit o' lime juice brought by Cap'n Earl's man, who said it were better than coffee when the sun was already hotter 'n whore's drawers."

Anthony took the glass and found the lime juice cool and sweetened. Not the usual sour taste he was used too.

Seeing Anthony peer at his glass Bart volunteered, "'e put a bit sugar into hit."

Anthony had left Silas aboard *Warrior* trying not to overcrowd *Merlin's* already close quarters. Earl's servant, an ole topman named Lamb, had done his best to please the admiral.

"Deck there!" The lookout called down, "Signal from *Audacity*, flotsam in the water."

Captain Earl turned to Lord Anthony, "Heave to?"

"Aye," Anthony replied, "and signal *SeaWolf* our intentions."

"Aye, aye, my lord. Mr. Scott, let's be getting the signals bent on."

Then before the midshipman could respond the lookout called down, "Deck there! Signal from *SeaWolf*, strange sail in sight."

Anthony could feel his adrenalin rise as his heart began to race. "Captain Earl, please disregard my last order to heave to and make all sail to yonder sighting. Signal *SeaWolf* to investigate strange sail, and then advise *Audacity* to follow after a look at the flotsam."

"Aye, my lord," Earl replied. He could feel a sense of excitement at the sighting of the sail.

"Deck there! Signal from *SeaWolf*, strange sail 'as went about and 'as headed back toward the east."

Bart looked at Lord Anthony, "To the Keys, do you think?"

"Aye, that's my thinking. Like a fox looking for a hole with the hounds at his heels."

Earl approached Anthony and said, "With the wind almost astern we could sail another point or two to starboard. Then maybe we can overhaul the chase.

From her present position she'll have to tack before she closes with the nearest Key and by that time it's possible we'll be in position to cut off her escape."

Nodding his agreement Anthony said, "She's your ship, captain, sail her as you think best." Then as an afterthought he added, "Signal *SeaWolf* your intention."

"Aye, my lord," Earl answered then went about ordering the change.

Within the turn of the glass it was obvious they were vastly overhauling the strange ship.

The lookout had called down, "She's 'as the cut of a Dago, zur."

Bart had also been eyeing the ship and turned to Anthony, "She's a big un. I bet she wuz a merchantman turned privateer and I'll bet she's loaded to the gills."

"Aye, Bart, my thoughts as well."

With *SeaWolf* and *Merlin* converging on the chase they'd soon be upon her. Captain Earl approached Anthony again, "Beat to quarters, my lord?"

"I think that would be appropriate."

Then to punctuate the order the lookout called down, "The chase 'as fired on *SeaWolf*, zur. No 'it as I can tell."

"Captain Earl?"

"Aye, my lord!"

"As soon as convenient and we are in range have the bow chasers put into action."

"Yes, my lord."

Bart had gone below and now he returned. "Your weapons, sir. I figured yew's be wanting us-uns to help out today."

"Not ready to leave the fighting to the younger tars," Anthony taunted his cox'n.

"Nay, my lord, maybe the exercise will do us-uns some good. Silas's cooking 'as turned us fat. Lady

Deborah won't 'ardly recognize yew wid yews girth 'spanding such."

"My girth," Anthony exclaimed, sucking in his stomach. "Damme Bart but you've taken on a portly appearance yourself."

"Well, maybe I 'as but it's a wise man wot builds a shed over 'is tools."

"What tools is that?" Anthony asked sarcastically.

"Me wedding tackle, that's wot tools."

"Humph!" Anthony snorted, "They're probably rusted off from lack of use by now."

Bart cocked his head and very stoically replied, "Nay, I use 'em regular like. Back in Saint Augustine they's this little mulatto who can't 'ardly wait till old Bart is there to dip 'is wick. She be a delightfully naughty little wench if they ever was one."

Not believing his ear, Anthony suddenly became serious. "Why Bart, I didn't know you had a steady woman. Is this more than just a fling with a trollop?"

"I ain't sure yet," Bart replied. "'Er daddy be Portuguese and 'er mother's Spanish, English and mulatto mixed. But even if it's just a touch, she still 'as a bit o' black in her. 'Eer daddy paid one hundred pounds for 'er mother. After seeing 'er I believes 'e got a bargain and Esmeralda is more beautiful than 'er mother."

"Is she for sale?" Anthony queried.

"I'm not sure," Bart replied, "I ain't got round to deciding iffen I wanta ask. It could be I could buy 'er, then it's possible 'er father would give 'er 'and in marriage. I just ain't decided if I's ready for a full time woman, 'specially with this war. She do make a good little bed warmer howsum ever."

The roar of the bowchaser sounded and broke up the conversation. The acrid smell of the smoke drifted aft as another shot was let loose from the bowchaser.

"Went through 'er mainsail," the lookout called down.

Taking his glass and resting it on a ratline Anthony looked at the distant ship. Gabe had ordered *SeaWolf* to let loose with her forward guns and now the chase was under fire from both ships.

"Captain Earl!"

"Yes, my lord."

"As soon as convenient I want you to load with grape. I'd like to board yonder ship if possible without having to face great odds."

"Aye, my lord," Earl replied, and then went about the admiral's order. He knew privateers tended to carry lots of extra men so his lordship was being prudent. It was not unheard of where a larger ship boarded a smaller vessel only to be swamped by all the extra men on board. Then it was the privateers who gained a prize and not the other way around.

The wind had veered somewhat and after three broadsides in less than two minutes *Merlin* was completely engulfed in smoke from her larboard cannons. However the chase was now firing back. A portion of the taffrail was hit and a sailor screamed as splinters flew through the air. Another ball hit amidships dismembering a man as it put a great gouge in *Merlin's* gun deck. A shout from forward caused Anthony to peer over the bulwark in time to see the chase's mainmast go tumbling over the side with a great crack not unlike a cannon firing.

However, the ship's captain was a stubborn if not wise man and he continued to fight for his ship. Only his forward guns could bear on *Merlin*; and *SeaWolf* had now crossed the ship's stern firing as she crossed.

Anthony could hear Bart saying, "That's me boy. Gabe put a ball up 'er arse and blowed out 'er innards. That'll slow 'em down I'm bettin'."

Slow the return fire it did, but still the captain of the chase showed no signs of surrendering.

Seeing Earl, Anthony ordered, "We'll grapple and board to starboard, signal *SeaWolf* to do the same to larboard."

"Aye, my lord," Earl replied then shouted out the orders.

Another broadside from *Merlin* sent grape buzzing through the chase like a wad of hornets.

Seeing *SeaWolf* close with the chase, Anthony then ordered Earl, "Have the gunners cease firing Captain. We don't want grape cutting down on *SeaWolf's* crew as they board."

"Aye, my lord. Mr. Campbell," Earl called to his first lieutenant, "have the cannons cease fire then prepare to board yonder ship."

The ships were coming together now and as the hulls ground together a shudder went through *Merlin* causing Anthony to stumble.

Bart caught a hold of him smiling and said, "No lying back now; it be time for that exercise yews been talking bout."

Then, with a pistol in one hand and a sword in the other, off the two went to join the melee. The sound of muskets filled Anthony's ears. Shots rang out as marine sharpshooters fired down on the men in the chase while a hand full of privateers fired back at the marines. A sergeant fell next to Anthony then struggled to his feet, blood pouring from a useless left arm.

One of the rogues on the chase lunged at Bart with a bayonet he'd picked up from a dead marine. The attack was clumsy and Bart easily parried the blade then slashed down with his cutlass, splitting the man's chest.

The fight became very close as screams, curses and words of encouragement all filled the air. Anthony knew the fight couldn't last long as the enemy ship had been boarded from both quarters and British sailors now had flooded the deck.

Another rascal had just attacked Anthony who deflected the blow but was thrown off balance in doing so. His attacker then thrust his blade forward, the tip of which stung as it pierced flesh entering Anthony's abdomen. Anthony twisted and avoided most of the man's attack, then raised his pistol and fired into the man's chest. Dropping the pistol to the deck, Anthony shifted his cutlass to his right hand and with his left pulled the blade from his flesh. Hot, warm blood flowed over his hand as he did so.

Seeing the admiral wounded, another foe attacked him only to have Bart step between the two. Surprise filled the man's face as an enraged Bart now in a killing mood smashed the hilt of his cutlass into the man's face; dazing his opponent who never saw the backward swing of Bart's blade that severed his head which toppled to the deck before the rest of the body slumped.

Standing over Anthony, Bart called, "*Merlin's,* to me, to the admiral."

The British sailors quickly gathered in a knot around their admiral to protect him, but the fight was over. Gabe was quickly there. After seeing to his brother, Gabe sent Dagan to fetch Caleb while he tried to make him comfortable. Anthony was carried to Earl's quarters on *Merlin* protesting that he could walk. Caleb quickly removed Anthony's coat and shirt. He gently probed the wound with a cloth soaked in rum. Then taking a clean rag Caleb ran it through the wound leaving a wick of sorts.

"Twisting as you did," Caleb explained, "the man's blade penetrated the fleshy part of the abdomen but did not enter the viscera. Therefore, the internal organs were not disturbed. I have ordered an anodyne…a nostrum composed of extraction Thebaicum and wine. It will induce sleep and prevent pain. A dose of which I think will be most needed once the adrenalin of the battle has waned. The only concern would be if the evil humours create a putrid fistula in the wound. If necessary a balm of sulfur, glycerin and hogs lard can be impregnated into a dressing and applied."

As the group left, Anthony gave Earl instructions about the captured ship. His words slurred from Caleb's concoction before he could complete his orders. The last words he heard before sleep overtook him was Bart saying, "I's didn't mean for you to loose yews belly that way."

Damn him, Anthony thought, *always has to have the last word.*

Chapter Seventeen

Damme, but I don't know what's worse, Lord Anthony thought. *This pain from the wound, nausea from Caleb's concoction or the headache from the hammering on deck.*

Earl had just come down to visit along with Gabe and the masters from each ship as ordered by Anthony.

"Repairs on *Merlin* and *SeaWolf* are about finished so we can soon be underway," Earl had said.

"We were lucky," Gabe had said.

Neither *Merlin* nor *SeaWolf* had anything other than superficial damage. The captured ship had at one time been a merchant vessel that had been converted into a privateer. She had been armed much like a forty gun frigate. She was old but still seaworthy. At the time of battle she only carried a crew of some two hundred.

However, even from the poor attempt at recordkeeping by her captain, it appeared she had started her cruise with some three hundred and seventy five men. Some of these men were recorded D.D. or discharged dead while others were noted to have been used as prize crews on captured ships. From the initials D.D., Anthony could only assume whoever had tried their hand at recordkeeping had spent some time in the British Navy.

The remaining privateer's crew appeared to be a mixture of Colonials, French, Spanish and even a few blacks. The records also showed an alarmingly large list of ships and cargos taken.

"Damned busy fellow if you ask me," Earl had said.

The name on the ship's stern was the *Argus* but the ship was definitely Spanish built. Dagan had talked to a few of her crew and they all seemed aware of a "Ghost ship" that deliberately destroyed rather than take its foe.

"She's called a ghost ship because all the captain leaves behind is the spirits of the dead souls he's sent to the deep. One of the men we questioned said once he's blasted away at the ships protecting the convoy, he'll send a boat to various ships. If a cargo strikes his fancy he'll take it but just as often he'll just stand off and fire into a ship until she's sunk, with no apparent rhyme or reason. Usually it's a ship what be under British colors."

All heads turned as Bart spoke. He generally didn't say much during a conference but when he did it paid to listen.

Lord Anthony looked at his cox'n and queried, "Where did you get this information?"

"From a rogue what 'ad run and signed on with the freebooters," Bart replied, "I see'd this man wot had tattoos on his arm and 'ad a Kentish accent. So I's sided up to 'em wid a wet and says we looking for good tars. I told 'em iffen he'd mind 'is manners like and was helpful in giving us-uns some useful 'telegence, life would go better for 'em. Utterwise 'ed be dancing the newgate jig for desertin'."

Bart's use of "newgate jig" to threaten a hanging caused a chuckle from the officers. "'Pears' he seed things me way," Bart continued, "'Cause after a taste of me wet his tongue loosened up quicker than a whore's drawers."

"Did the scoundrel say where the ship's homeport is?" Anthony asked.

"He's not sure," Bart continued, "They've seen 'em at Isla de Tesoros and at Cayo Hueso."

"Where are these places?" Anthony asked directing his question to the two masters.

"I know more about Cayo Hueso than Isla de Tesoros," Gunnells replied.

"What about you, Quinn?" he asked Earl's master.

"I've been to Isla de Tesoros," Quinn replied. "Its name means Treasure Island after all the loot what's been cached there over the years. It's a small island that lies under Havana's belly. There's several smaller islands scattered about. There's no way to get close without being spotted except for a night passage. Something I'd be leery of. My charts are sketchy at best, but the passage from either the eastern or western side is narrow with reefs and small islands that could ground or worse rip the bottom clean out of a vessel. I'd not try without a pilot. If that's his lair I'd blockade the area."

"We can't," Earl interrupted, "That would create a national incident."

"We still may take a peek," Anthony replied not yet ready to give up. He then turned his attention back to Gunnells, "Tell me about Cayo Hueso."

"It used to be called Bone Key from all the dead Indians that died in a big Indian War," Gunnells said, "Now it's called Cayo Hueso which is Dago for Key West. It's a small island about three and one-half by one and one-half miles. My charts say it's the deepest port between New Orleans in the Gulf and Norfolk in the Atlantic. Due to the abundant rainfall there's usually plenty of fresh water. The island is full of small inlets that wind their way into thick stands of mangroves. There are also lots of mahogany trees that are good for ship's repair. Far as I know while both Havana and Britain claim it, no one government controls it. It's used by fishermen to dry and salt their catch. There's more'n one story of wreckers luring some ship in only to run aground. While the port is deep water it'd take a skilled man to navigate the treacherous reefs and currents. Somebody like your flag lieutenant."

"My flag lieutenant?" Anthony quizzed with a surprised look on his face.

"Aye, my lord. We've shared a wet at the Mermaid and he told me before the war he'd done a bit o'...salvage work."

"Well, damme," Anthony exclaimed, "Maybe Dagan's lady luck has decided to smile down upon us."

Then almost as an afterthought Anthony asked, "Did anyone get a name for this ghost ship?"

"Aye," Bart spoke up again, "She be the *Barracuda*."

"Hummph...," Anthony mused. "Is there anything to suggest the *Argus* and *Barracuda* are in link."

"No, my lord, just the opposite I would say," Earl answered. "Unlike the organization we found with the captain of the *Reaper*, the *Barracuda* has chosen the name well. She appears to be a rogue ship that for the most part operates alone. A ship that has a vendetta for the British."

At this point the sentry announced, "*Merlin's* first lieutenant says winds picking up." Upon hearing this, the two masters made their way topside. Gabe said his good-byes and departed as well.

"Did you find anything else of interest on the *Argus*?" Anthony asked Earl after everyone was gone.

"Not really, sir. Stores were almost depleted so I believe the ship was headed to replenish them. I was amazed at the variation and amounts of specie...hard specie that was found. There was a chest full of specie from every nation, silver livres, gold louis, guineas, pistoles, dollars, all hard coins, no paper at all my lord."

"Humph!" Anthony grunted, "You must have made it to the captain's cabin before Dagan got there."

"Sir," Earl asked, not quite sure what to make of Anthony's words.

"I said you must have searched the captain's cabin before Dagan had a chance."

"Oh no, my lord. It was he that found the specie."

Nodding his head in understanding Anthony said, "Well you can damn well bet you only got half at best."

"Half sir?"

"Yes, man, half," Anthony spoke sharply as the pain from his wound was getting more bothersome. "You can be sure Dagan got all he could carry before you were notified of its existence."

"Oh! I catch your drift, sir. Do we search Dagan's belongings?"

Anthony just looked up at Earl with a hard look that spoke volumes even though he was silent.

Seeing the look Earl said, "No, I don't believe there's a need to embarrass Dagan. I don't see how he could have appropriated any significant amount of the booty without my knowledge."

"If you're sure," Anthony said, "then it's a moot point. I have nothing but the utmost in trust and confidence in my captains so your word is good enough for me."

Earl suddenly looked anxious. He rose from his seat, gulped down the wine in his glass then suddenly remembered he was needed on deck. As he left the cabin Bart came out of the pantry, "Smart bugger, ain't he?"

"Bart!"

"Aye, my lord, I know's he's a King's ozzifer and a smart un to boot I'm thinking."

Anthony quickly recovered from his injuries once they returned to Saint Augustine. He refused the bosun chair when going back on board *Warrior*, but by the time he made it up the ladder and through the entry port he was wishing he hadn't let pride get in the way of comfort.

Captain Buck was taken aback by Anthony's pale flesh tones and stooped position as he walked. Once in his stateroom Silas had a cup of his special coffee ready for the admiral, then went about making Anthony comfortable as he laid down on his day bed. Captain Earl and his ship's surgeon had accompanied the admiral over to the flagship. *Merlin's* surgeon was explaining to *Warrior's* surgeon Caleb's plan of treatment for the admiral.

"The man's treating the admiral and he's not even in the Navy," *Merlin's* surgeon exclaimed.

Standing to the side Bart was amazed to hear the conversation. It appeared the two ship's surgeons were somewhat in awe at Caleb's plan of care.

"I would have bled him a pint at least," Johnson, who was *Warrior's* surgeon, said.

"Nay," McBain, from *Merlin* answered. "Caleb says the depletion of volume stresses the cardium and prevents the sanguine suppuration which delivers the humours from the wound."

Damn me ears, Bart thought. *I don't need to be listening to this but if I's ever wounded I hope Caleb is handy.*

Anthony sipped his coffee patiently until the two surgeons finished addressing his wound. He politely stated, "Now if you gentlemen will forgive me I have duties to discuss with the flag captain."

Once the surgeons had left, Anthony moved around until he found a relaxing position. He then turned to Buck and asked, "Has anything of interest developed while I was gone?"

"We had a day of strong wind and rain. Enough that the master wanted to up anchor and put some distance between us and the land."

Shaking his head in understanding Anthony recalled his recent conversation with the Governor, "*If it came a blow they would have to put to sea.*"

"Did you hear me, sir?" Buck asked.

"My apologies Rupert, my mind was on the weather and this damnable anchor. You were saying?"

"I was saying, sir, that Knight and Markham had a running battle with a group of privateers but lost them after the sun went down. Knight thinks they made it into one of the many inlets between Port Royal and Savannah. Markham wanted to explore a likely place feeling that with *Swan's* shallow draught he could put a man in the chains and get a look see."

"However, since *Neptune* was too large to follow and render assistance should it be needed, Knight denied Markham's request."

"Sir Raymond is a wise officer," Anthony said.

"Aye, my lord, I believe a few of our younger captains have succeeded until it may now prove to be a liability," Buck said.

"Meaning Francis and Gabe?" Anthony asked.

"Aye," Buck answered matter-of-factly. "Them along with Bush and Kerry. That damn fool stunt of Kerry's, taking on a gunboat off Nova Scotia had disaster written all over it. Bart was right when he said, "Brave man, Mister Kerry is, but not the smartest block I've known."

Anthony smiled in spite of himself recalling the day. "I didn't know Bart's words had got out."

Now Buck was smiling, "Got out, my lord! Why they're damn near legendary," Buck exclaimed. "Bart summed up the feeling of every tar in the whole squadron with that one sentence. And with him being the admiral's own cox'n! Why damn my eyes, sir, but most of the officers felt the same as Bart but wouldn't say it.

Over the next few days the number of ships entering port increased until the anchorage and even the harbour was bustling. Ships delivering their cargo of precious supplies that would be needed to maintain the force at Saint Augustine until after the hurricane season.

Anthony kept up the patrols and *Merlin* in company with *SeaWolf* and *Audacity* had driven off a group of privateers attempting to raid the convoy that had just dropped anchor. A dilapidated xebec had been taken prize.

Where in God's name had that come from, Anthony wondered.

Earl had said when he reported, "She's an old craft, sir, her batteries were mounted with the refuse guns off some Frenchy's old, rusty relic's that had long since served their real usefulness. I'm surprised they didn't blow to pieces when they were fired."

"Well," Anthony said, "maybe the Governor will have a use for her so that she'll make the jacks a farthing or two."

Earl then silenced his admiral and flag captain as he continued, "The captain of the xebec was Spanish, sir. He was mortally wounded in the battle but he was still able to talk when we boarded. He was in fact in a rage and damned us all to hell for stealing his home and his land. I didn't put much stock in his ranting until in a fit of coughing he gasped "you were nothing but bait for the *Barracuda* and Don Luis de Lavago." The crew of the xebec was a mixed bunch. With a little persuading we discovered from a man who is most assuredly a British deserter, but claims to be Canadian, that Captain

Galvez... Cesar Galvez, was always complaining of losing his plantation in Cow Ford."

"Humph!" Anthony grunted when Earl had finished his report. "I will bet herein lies the reason for the ruthless destruction of British ships. A Spaniard or Spaniards who were probably forced by circumstances, cultural differences, or any number of reasons to relocate to Cuba after the treaty between Spain and England."

"Aye," Buck said, "A man with a vendetta. I wonder if we could find out more of either Captain Galvez or Don..."

"Don Luis de Lavago," Earl added. "Gabe and I discussed this when we captured the xebec and he said with your permission, sir, he would see if he could find anything out from Domingo."

"Yes...yes, that would be useful," Anthony replied after a moment of thought. "I understand he is a man of much knowledge."

Hearing this Buck added, "He's a man with a beautiful daughter as well, my lord. Keeps our Sir Raymond in a fit of humours."

"Not just Sir Raymond," Earl added, "But I believe he's won Nancy's heart if not her hand. I'm not sure how that will play out but I wouldn't be surprised to see a Lady Knight in the not to distant future."

"Would a priest be willing to do that?" Anthony questioned. "Sir Raymond's a Protestant."

"A sea captain could," Buck interjected, "If Domingo approved."

That night Gabe spent time talking with his friend and business partner. Since the incident with Lancaster, the tavern had become something of a "hangout" for the warrants and officers in Anthony's squadron. Business was better than it had ever been and Domingo for once had realized a substantial profit. Gabe had earned a tidy sum himself and though he hadn't told Domingo as yet he intended to turn sole ownership of the tavern back over to the man when orders came for his ship. Tonight over a glass of sangria they talked of Don Luis de Lavago.

"Si, my compadre, I know of him. He was a very rich aristocrat from Madrid. Only he was the second son. He had accumulated much though. He owned...how you say it, mucho land along the Saint Johns River all the way to Cowford. Much time and expense had been made and when he's at the point to make mucho dinero England suddenly owns all his land and holdings with nothing for all his expense and labors. Havana had nothing to offer that would equal his loss I am told. Now he is a violent, sick man with much hatred. He hates all gringos. No offense, señor."

"None taken," Gabe assured Domingo.

"Don Luis hates all whites but because his cause and needs are the same as the rebels to the north he has, on occasion, formed a loose allegiance. If they win the war it is said his former holding will be returned by the rebels. Who knows? It is too much for Domingo to consider."

This, Gabe believed. Like thousands of people at home who believed the war was Lord North's doings and the only people who would benefit from the war would be the rich, not the common man.

Chapter Eighteen

The sun was blood red and high in the sky. *Neptune*, *Swan* and *Pigeon* sailed southward under a lazy wind and unwavering glare. To look upon the shining water made your eyes hurt. Deck seams were so sticky that they gripped to a man's foot.

Knight had just seen a sailor jump as barefooted he stepped on a bubble of tar. Leaning against the bulwark he could feel the heat off the adjacent cannon. The barrels were as hot as if they had been in battle.

Lord Anthony was acting upon information he'd recently received that the privateer ship *Barracuda* was seen operating off the southern tip of Florida and the Keys. There seemed to be some idea as to who the cutthroat was that commanded the *Barracuda* but when the patrol had sailed nothing more definite had been found out.

Feeling sticky and clammy Knight called to his first lieutenant, "Mr. Brooks, I'm going to my cabin to sign some papers. The master has promised a shower this afternoon and I don't think a little cooling off would be amiss. However, keep a close eye out for squalls as well as sails and call me if you need me."

Before the "aye, captain" was out of Brooks mouth Knight's head disappeared down the companion ladder.

After an hour or so of working at his desk Knight felt the motion of the ship become a bit livelier and at the same time realized the cabin had become dimmer and the sun didn't seem to penetrate the stained glass in the stern windows as it had an hour ago. Returning on deck he could instantly feel a sharp stinging rain.

"I was just sending the midshipman for you, sir," Lieutenant Brooks volunteered, "although our good master says this will only last an hour or so."

"Well," Knight answered as the rain pelted away at his thin shirt, "if it cools things down it will be worth a little dampness."

As is the usual for his breed the master was right on the mark. "Fifty-five minutes by me watch," he exclaimed as suddenly the rain ceased.

"Land ho, off the starboard bow," the lookout called down.

There was an island just making itself visible as the clouds cleared from the sky. Sunlight beat across the deck on the damp planking and large drops from the recent squall dripped down from the rigging leaving dark circles on the deck that dried quickly.

"Deck there," the lookout called down, "sails just off yonder island."

Before Knight could digest this information Lieutenant Brooks was at his side, "Signal from *Pigeon*, sir, requests permission to investigate."

"Permission granted," Knight replied. *Pigeon* had been on station to starboard and therefore was between *Neptune* and the Keys. Meanwhile Markham had *Swan* on station to larboard of *Neptune*.

The sail turned out to be a small lugger and the captain had ignored the signal to heave to, so *Pigeon* was trying to overhaul the small ship. Watching as the lugger made its way through a channel heading into the Keys, Lieutenant Kerry of *Pigeon* was daydreaming. He loved his little ketch but he longed for something bigger, something like *SeaWolf.* Now that was a command to have. Damned if he wouldn't be able to put away a bit of prize money if he commanded a ship so fine.

Suddenly, Kerry was awakened from his daydreams. Why hadn't he been paying attention…now he'd put his ship in danger. Things were happening…something awful. He found himself flying through the air in a torrent of flames and splinter that stung like a thousand needles all at once then as he hit the waters, just before everything went black he heard the explosion that ruined his dream.

Standing on deck, *Neptune's* officers watched unbelieving at the ruthless barrage of cannon fire pouring into the tiny ship. The flashing orange tongues seem to leap out from the seemingly peaceful mangrove trees. The *Barracuda* had been lying in wait and the lugger had been the bait. Knight could see the waterspouts bursting all around the *Pigeon* as the cannon's flames spit forth from the hidden ship.

"Mr. Brooks?"

"Aye, aye captain."

"Beat to quarters and signal *Swan,* though damme I hope Markham is faster responding than I've been."

Markham on board *Swan* had heard and seen the onslaught of cannon fire that tore into the helpless ketch. Using his glass as *Swan* closed with the Keys, Markham could see men running frantically about with gesturing arms.

Some were hacking away at the downed mast and spar, while others were gallantly firing *Pigeon's* popguns at the ghost ship that was so entwined with the trees and vegetation she was not even clearly visible. Meanwhile, *Neptune* was closely approaching the scene. Knight had ordered the bow chasers to open fire as soon as they were in range. The boom of the bow chaser was quickly answered by a cry from the lookout.

"Last shot was over *Pigeon* but the enemy ship is showing 'er heels."

The forward guns continued to fire and the lookout called down again, "A 'it by gawd. The last ball sent splinters a flying as we pounded one up 'er arse."

The master was now in front of Knight, "We're to close, captain. We need to anchor now and send in boats. I can see weeds off to larboard."

"Very well," Knight replied. "Heave to. There has to be a channel, possibly one that continues to the other side, where the cutthroat is escaping."

"However, we'll heave to and render what help we can," Knight said with defeat in his voice.

Before they could get the boats in the water *Swan* was alongside, Markham joined Knight in his gig as they rowed toward the helpless ship. As they got close the cries of pain and anguish could be heard.

Mr. Davy who was standing in the bow of a longboat that was alongside Knight's gig spoke out, "She's on a sandbar. That's why she hasn't sunk."

Davy was right. *Pigeon* had come to rest on a sandbar having been leered into position where the *Barracuda* had been silently waiting. Markham's knuckles turned white as he grasped the side of the gig. Knight sat across from Markham trying to shut out the human agony that confronted him. His recent bout with the privateer's attack at Saint Augustine all too fresh in his memory not to feel the hell the crew on *Pigeon* must be feeling.

Men's bodies were so badly mutilated it was hard to realize they had once been human. A sailor grabbed a rope that was heaved by the bowman. As he stood the sight of his breeches spattered with blood and gore made the bowman retch.

"Don't worry," cried the sailor. "I t ain't mine!"

The chorus of cries and groans on board as men stumbled about was heart wrenching. Men were lying with open mouths and open dead eyes. A man seemed to shudder then slumped forward. Mr. Davy pulled at the man who fell back half his face gone, the other half covered in dark congealed blood.

The *Pigeon* was listing badly. Great sections of the once beautiful ketch floated on the tide. Men were working to cut the mainmast adrift as it thumped against the battered hull. Of the fifty-five men who crewed *Pigeon* only a handful were not wounded and able to perform their full duties while another half dozen were walking wounded. When *Neptune's* surgeon had made his way on *Pigeon's* deck he had declared, "Not much work for me, a chaplain maybe but not me."

Once the survivors were removed Knight had charges laid about. "I'll not see her scavenged," he said to Markham. There was precious little to scavenge thought Markham but he agreed. The explosion that sent swells under the boats being rowed back to their ships was ignored by the men. Not one turned to see the little ship slip away below the surface as she and her dead came to their final resting place.

Admiral Anthony and Flag Captain Buck sat quietly at the admiral's table. Bart and Silas were silent in the pantry and Flag Lieutenant Hazard stood to the back of Admiral Anthony, moisture filling his eyes as Knight made his solemn report. Markham stood by quietly reliving the moment as Knight explained in detail the loss of Lieutenant Kerry and *HMS Pigeon*. As usual the word had spread throughout the squadron and created a somber mood. Everyone had known and liked the captain of the lost ship and its crew.

"I'm sorry, my lord," Knight said as he finished his report. "I shouldn't have allowed Kerry to venture in as he did."

"Sorry...why damme sir it's I who should be sorry. I should have brought this rogue to play before now. Captain Buck."

"Aye, my lord."

"General signal to the squadron, prepare for sea."

"The entire squadron, my lord?" Buck asked.

"Yes, put every ship a sail. We're going fishing...for *Barracuda*."

Anthony reported to Tonyn and made him aware of his plan.

"But what of Saint Augustine, what are we to do?"

"You have both the *Rose* and the captured xebec," Anthony answered diplomatically. "But in truth, sir, I believe the knowledge of us being here has been spread so that no attempt on the city is likely. We will probably be back before the word can be spread that we're gone. I also believe once we deal with the *Barracuda* the menace will be so reduced there'll be no need for an entire squadron."

"We'll see," Tonyn answered skeptically, but he did agree the *Barracuda* had to be dealt with and soon.

For six long days Anthony's squadron sailed down the coast of Florida and into the Keys. The cutter, *Audacity*, was used to take soundings and mark channels in and around the Keys where a ship could hide. Lieutenant Hazard was on board acting as a pilot to help mark the channels on the admiralty chart. It felt good being back at sea doing something useful...something he'd spent his life before the Navy doing.

At the larger Keys men went ashore in boats. At Key Largo a large fishing village was found where the fisherman admitted seeing the large ship captained by a Spaniard. He was last seen at Long Key the man had said, but he was also seen at Sugarloaf Key and Cayo Hueso. Cayo Hueso is much in use.

"Lots of pirates hide in that area," the man had said. "They call it Pirates Cove. It has a deep water anchorage and therefore many ships stop there. This makes for big profit for the pirates."

After hearing this Anthony set down with Buck and Oxford, *Warrior's* old master. "Looking at these charts," Anthony said, "it looks like it's only a small distance from Cayo Hueso to Havana."

"Aye, my lord, about ninety to one hundred odd miles I'd say."

"And to Isla de Tesoros?" Anthony queried.

"I'd double that and more," the master said. "You have to sail around the western tip of Cuba from our current position."

"Yes, I remember," Anthony said. Then turning to Buck, he said, "I think we'll poke our nose into Havana Harbour. Just enough for them to know that we're about."

"Might flush out a rat," Oxford said.

"Or a *Barracuda*," Buck chimed in.

"Might not either." This interruption made the three men look up from the chart. Anthony knew something was amiss the way Bart had spoken. Once he had their attention, Bart continued, "We just got a signal from Gabe, water spout on the horizon and the sky is turning dark."

"Gawd!" Buck exclaimed.

The group then made their way on deck.

"Aye, we're in for a blow," Oxford said in a nervous voice as he went to check the barometer. "Pressure is falling," he stated matter-of-factly.

Buck then turned to Anthony and could see the conflict going on in his mind. Command…so much responsibility; not just one ship but the entire squadron. Without thinking Buck touched Anthony's arm.

Glaring at the darkening sky Anthony said, "I know Rupert. We can't be caught here in a blow. Make general signal, take position on flag, and then set a course for Saint Augustine. The *Barracuda* will live to swim another day, but not for long."

As Anthony walked dejectedly back to his cabin Buck thought, *Damn the Dago bastard anyway!*

PART III

Return to Port

Rain falls when it wants to,
Like the wind that fills our sail.
I recall the tears on her face,
When we said our farewells.
Her memory's like a dagger,
The blade, cold and sharp.
All the nights I walked these decks,
With a lonely aching heart.
Tomorrow we'll return to port;
This cruise is finally over.
She'll be standing on the pier,
Waiting for me to hold her.

-Michael Aye

Chapter Nineteen

The storm lashed out violently as the waves crashed and beat upon the wooden hull of the ships in Lord Anthony's squadron. The pennant snapped and sounded like a gunshot as the mast and spars groaned. The winds created a whistling sound in the shrouds as the storm blasted down on the ships.

The helmsman steered a course almost due north as the squadron tried to outrun the tempest. It was on the eve of the third day the sun peeked through the clouds and the wind that drove the ships so furiously quieted down to a gentle breeze. Anthony came on deck and greeted his flag captain.

"She's a gallant ship, captain."

"Aye, my lord, with a gallant crew. It is my intent to splice the main brace before we come about and make our way to Saint Augustine."

"Good idea," Anthony replied. "How's the rest of the squadron?"

"All present and on station," Buck replied. "*Audacity* looks a little worse for wear but she's under full sail." Then Buck looking past his admiral could see the master approaching. "Well, Mr. Oxford, have you a good guess for our position?"

Anthony smiled appreciatively. Oxford would be as close as anybody could be but Buck was right. The exact position would be little more than a good guess until the noon sights could be done on the morrow.

Oxford ignored Buck's remarks and said, "There's a group of islands to larboard that I think is the Outer Banks of North Carolina so I judge we're in fact just off Cape Hatteras."

The master's positioning was very accurate as was usual for his breed of old salts. After the noon sighting the following day the squadron came about and made a leisurely cruise south to Saint Augustine. *Audacity* and *SeaWolf* chased a small schooner up the Cape Fear River inlet before being recalled by the flagship. Lord Anthony also allowed *Swan* and *SeaWolf* to take a peek into the harbour at Charlestown and Savannah but found nothing in either place.

The sight of British men-o'-war did cause alarm to the citizens of both places whose life had been very peaceful up to that point. It was at sundown on the fourth day after coming about the squadron dropped anchor at Saint Augustine.

Lord Anthony was disgusted as he seemed to face nothing but one frustration after another in his attempt to come to grips with the privateer *Barracuda*.

"We have been very successful overall," Buck pointed out. "Our convoys are making it through so there's no doubt as to our impact."

"Aye," Lord Anthony agreed, "but I'll not rest until *Pigeon* is avenged. We cannot, I will not allow a ship under my command to be destroyed without bringing the offender to justice."

Buck could tell by Anthony's voice his ire was up.

"They have to know," Anthony said his arm making a sweeping motion, "that to destroy a King's ship is to doom their fate. I will not rest until the rogue is brought to bear."

Bart was standing inside the pantry with Silas. Anthony's words were easily overheard. "I's 'spect that cap'n of the *Barracuda* is in a fix."

"Aye," Silas answered, "His days be numbered alright. When his lordship gets 'is temper up somebody generally pays."

"Me thoughts as well," Bart answered. "Don Louis is a dead man and 'e jus' don't know it yet."

"Aye," Silas agreed, "not yet 'e don't, but soon."

No sooner had the ships dropped anchor than Governor Tonyn's secretary came aboard with new orders for Lord Anthony. After reading his orders Anthony had Sir Raymond and Gabe repair on board. When all had settled on board and Silas had served a glass of refreshment for the group Anthony got down to business.

"The rebels are sending another invasion force into Florida. We have this on good word. The force is said to contain more than one thousand troops. Governor Tonyn is taking this as a very serious threat. He has already sent a force under Colonel Provost to repel the attack. However, we are to land a group of scouts under Colonel Browne at Cowford just north of here. Gabe, as *SeaWolf* has the shallowest draught you will put into the mouth of the Saint Johns River here," Anthony said pointing at a place on the chart which was spread across the dining table. "Once at this place you will disembark Colonel Browne and his scouts and return here and maintain patrol along with *Neptune*."

"May I ask a question my lord?" Sir Raymond asked.

Glancing up Lord Anthony nodded his consent.

"If it's only a handful of scouts we're landing why are you sending both *SeaWolf* and *Neptune*?"

"Good question. There's a possibility some of the invasion force may come by sea...a two-pronged attack if you will. Therefore you will act as defender should difficulties arise."

"Aye my lord, we will be ready."

Gabe had barely made it back to *SeaWolf* and informed his first lieutenant and master of their orders when the boat carrying the scouts was sighted.

"Tis but a wee outing," Gunnells said as he quickly reviewed the charts prior to setting sail. The scouts were as motley a mixture as Gabe had ever seen. The group was made up of four blacks, seventeen whites, and the rest were Indians. They were dressed in a mixture of buckskin, homespun Lindsey Woolsey and breechcloths. Their outward appearance gave little hint to the effectiveness of the group.

Colonel Browne gave an air of competence and energy. In his late thirties or early forties he had made a reputation of being very skilled in the art of guerrilla warfare. This skill had not gone unnoticed by Governor Tonyn who had placed Browne in command of the East Florida Rangers. Browne was a man that was easy to like. He grew his hair long to cover the baldness where the Colonials had scalped him. Not only was he a soldier of merit Gabe decided but he was also a man set on retribution towards those who were responsible for his disfigurement.

Gabe glanced at the darkening sky as the anchorage became overcast. A zephyr carried the fresh smell of rain.

"Time for our afternoon shower," Dagan volunteered. "It'll not last."

"So you've become accustomed to the afternoon showers," Colonel Browne said, more a statement than a question.

"Do you wish for your men to go below," Gabe asked.

"No, captain, they're used to the elements. I'll not spoil them."

"As you wish," Gabe replied. He then called, "Mr. Jackson."

"Aye, captain."

"Prepare to get underway."

"Aye, sir." Jackson then ordered. "Man the capstan."

The sound of a fiddle on the fo'c'sle rang out. Lum had proved very talented musically as well as in other ways. Since arriving in Saint Augustine he had traded a handmade flute for a fiddle. He quickly learned to play it and now sawed a sassy tune.

"Jump to it you idle bugger," Graf shouted at the men. "Stir your stumps you whoresons. *Neptune's* anchor already has hove short. Damme but a sloven crew ye be."

"Anchors hove short," Lavery called from forward, his voice loud on a blustery wind as raindrops spattered on the decking stinging ones face as it pelted down.

"Get the ship underway, Jem," Gabe said using Jackson's first name. Pleased, Jackson turned to do as he was bid.

"Anchor's aweigh," Lavery shouted.

"Make sail," Jackson ordered. "Aloft sail loosners."

"Look lively now," Graf roared. Snap, the sound of Graf's starter against the main mast. "Foley the next un will be across your arse you laggard. Lay out and loosen, that's it me lads, stand by. Let fall, let fall, I say. Man the topsail sheets and halyard. Tend the braces."

As the evolution for getting underway was being completed *SeaWolf* was like a racehorse straining at the bit. Then as the sails were sheeted home she was off with a sudden surge that rocked the deck as they became underway. The scouts had not expected the sudden slanting of the deck and several found themselves bruised and aching after tumbling across the deck. This brought laughter from one of the seamen and caused the scouts to glare menacingly at the man.

"I say, Mr. Jackson," Gabe said. "See that yonder man is detailed to cleaning the heads for the next fortnight."

"Aye, sir, we'll see how much humour he finds in that."

Once clear of the anchorage the sea became more violent. Spray flew over the dipping bow and dashed scouts and seamen alike. A look of concern filled the scouts and so it was no surprise to Gabe when Colonel Browne approached him.

"It may be best, captain, if I accede to your previous offer for my men to go below. It'll be difficult for them to perform our mission if they've been knocked about so."

"I think your being wise, colonel," Gabe replied. "I find it taxing to ride horses so do not be embarrassed by being out of your element."

"Mr. Graf."

"Aye, cap'n."

"See to it that our guests are made comfortable below."

"Aye, cap'n, comfortable they'll be."

"Bye the mark five."

It had been a quick trip from Saint Augustine north to the entrance of the Saint Johns River. Knight in

Neptune sailed back and forth at the entrance as *SeaWolf* made its way up the river.

"Put our best leadsman in the chains," Gabe had ordered.

"Already done, sir," Jackson replied.

"Thank God we've such a shallow draught," a nervous Gunnells volunteered.

"*A quarter less five.*"

"Hell's fire," Gunnells again, "Maybe we should anchor and send the longboats the rest of the way."

The sails flapped loosely as the wind dropped.

"*By the mark four.*"

"Sir," Gunnells cried the anxiety apparent in his voice, "are we to loose our keel?"

"Bring her up another point," Gabe ordered, ignoring the master's pleas.

"We're shoaling fast," Jackson said.

"Nay," Dagan spoke out, "it'll be deeper ahead."

"I wish I had your confidence," Gunnells said, still very anxious.

"*Deep six.*"

There was a sigh of relief from Gunnells and a look of "I told you" from Dagan.

"*Deep eight,*" the leadsman called again.

The river widened at this point. On both sides of the river oak trees and scrubs were so thick it was hard to imagine a man being able to make his way through the dense vegetation. After rounding another bend, Dagan sided up to Gabe.

"I get the feeling we should heave to now."

Gabe started to argue but something in Dagan's demeanor made him forget his objections.

"Very well. Prepare to come about and anchor, Mr. Jackson."

"Aye sir."

"Mr. Graf."

"Aye, cap'n."

"Have the cutter and a longboat lowered."

"Mr. Lavery."

"Aye, sir."

"As soon as convenient convey our passengers ashore. Select a master's mate to be in charge of the longboat and return when your task is complete."

"Aye, sir."

The sun was dipping and as it set beyond the horizon strange noises arose from the forest. While the sun was down the humidity was still high and the men were soaked in sweat.

"Glad I ain't pulling one of those boats," Dagan said.

As the night came on and the air cooled ever so slightly a mist rose from the warm Saint Johns. The mist gave an eerie sensation. A slap forward was heard as a man defended himself from a determined mosquito. This made Gabe recall his recent trip up river to Savannah. They'd be no pipes tonight, however."

It was then Gabe realized all the sounds that dominated the night had suddenly ceased. No more sounds of crickets, no sounds of frogs, no sounds came from the forest; a sudden silence. The men on deck sensed the change as well. Mates spoke in nervous whispers if they spoke at all.

"Mr. Jackson," Gabe hissed.

"Aye, sir," the first lieutenant answered softly.

"Quietly, quietly mind you, have the men man the guns."

"Aye, sir," Jackson replied as he went to do his bidding.

Tension filled the air as weapons were laid out.

"See what the cook can fix the men," Gabe told Dagan, knowing it wouldn't be much with the galley fires out. "Mr. Jackson, after the men are fed let them sleep if they can but we'll remain at quarters."

Off to larboard a splash was heard. Was it a fish, or perhaps a bird after a fish. After awhile the wind shifted and the faint smell of wood smoke from somewhere inland drifted on the light breeze. "At least it'll help wid dem skeeters," Gabe heard Lum say but to whom was uncertain as the darkened deck seemed to be filled with shadows. The incoming tide created a lazy roll to the ship not unlike the rocking of a cradle.

Damme but this is not what SeaWolf was built for, thought Gabe.

Two hours had passed when Dagan nudged Gabe. Without realizing it Gabe had drifted off to sleep in spite of the pesky mosquitoes. He had been dreaming of swimming in a warm pool of water with Faith...nude. Then Dagan woke him. *Damme,* he thought, *this type of dream hadn't happened before and to be awakened before...ah.*

"I hear the boats coming," Dagan whispered. "They're pulling hard."

Gabe peered over the side but could see absolutely nothing in the mist, then almost like magic the cutter appeared followed by the longboat.

No sooner had the cutter ground to a halt than Lavery was through the entry port making his report, "Had it not been for the campfires we'd have rowed right into an ambush. One of the Colonel's Indians smelt the smoke so we went ashore. The Colonel had one of his scouts shimmy up a tree. The campfires were obvious from his advantage. I wanted to land the rangers there and head back," Lavery explained, "but the Colonel wanted to get closer and said it could be done more quickly and with less noise if we continued on the river. We pulled to a spot not more than twenty-five yards from where some of the rebels sat around their fires. I guess the Colonel could tell I was nervous about our being seen as close as we were. He told me not to worry. See the men staring into the fire? This has ruined their night vision. When they look away everything appears black. Let this be a lesson to you lad the Colonel said."

"If you are on bivouac put your back to the fire otherwise someone like my scouts will slit your throat before you can blink your eye. He sent one of his men to look for sentries and while we were sitting there we could hear the men at the fires talking. They already have five hundred or so men already staged, sir, but they are expecting another five hundred tomorrow…ere, this morning, sir. They are to come by sea, and run up this river in boats to meet up with those who came overland."

Hearing this disturbing news Gunnells spoke before the question was raised. "We are on the end of the ebb tide and the wind is outta the east, blowing directly against us. It'll be two hours is me guess before we can sail."

"Damme, what I'd give for a set of sweeps right now," Gabe cursed.

"Bit like a frog wishing for wings so 'e don't bump his arse," Gunnells said. Then seeing Gabe's look, apologized. "Sorry sir, didn't mean to be disrespectful."

"No offense taken," Gabe assured his master, "but we are up a creek without a paddle and I've a bad feeling about the morrow."

"I understand sir."

As the master ambled off Gabe called to Jackson, "Roust out the cook and light the galley fires. I want the men to have a good meal in them, so they'll be ready to face whatever the sunrise brings."

It could be they'd have to face the enemy on both fronts. Could Sir Raymond hold off the invasion force until they arrived to help? Lots of questions but no answers, Gabe thought

Chapter Twenty

Dawn was breaking as Sir Raymond Knight looked over the deck of *Neptune*. She was a fine ship with a fine crew. Knight glanced from one group of seamen to another. It hadn't been that long ago he'd been a first lieutenant and he would have been assigning duties to the warrants and petty officers.

Now it was different. More so than he would have imagined as a first lieutenant. He'd expected the responsibility that went with command but the isolation. That was the hard part. The part he had not considered or expected. The much sought after privacy of the captain's cabin also meant loneliness. Being "the captain" certainly meant privilege but there was also the burden. He had still not gotten over the destruction of the ketch *Pigeon* and the loss of Lieutenant Kerry. Should he have denied permission for him to give chase to that lugger. No, his mission had been to gather information and so the order was correct but it was a lesson...a lesson he'd not soon forget. Not all was as it might appear. Knight thrust his hands behind his back grasping the waistband of his trousers as he paced the weather side of the deck.

The air was already warm and humid and made his shirt stick to his chest. The wind teased his graying hair.

As the sun rose further shadows disappeared and the coast began to take shape. *How was Gabe getting along?* he wondered. If all went well he should be sighted soon. They'd heard no commotion during the night to suggest otherwise.

"Sail ho, dead astern," the lookout called down. "She be a big un zur."

Then before Knight could think another cry from above, "Two ships astern, zur, in close company. The second appears to be the *Barracuda*."

Hell's teeth, Knight thought, *where's SeaWolf?...though precious little help she'd be.*

"Mr. Brooks."

"Aye, captain."

"Beat to quarters if you please. It's a hot time we're about to have I'm thinking."

"Do we come about, sir?" Brooks asked.

"Aye," Knight replied sarcastically, "it's a fight we're in for, but I'll not let the buggers sodomize us as well."

This brought a chuckle from the second lieutenant until a glare from Knight cut it off.

"Mr. Dey."

"Aye," the second lieutenant answered solemnly after being silently rebuked.

"Yonder ships would like to have us between them but I'm not giving them the pleasure. We may have to pass them consecutively but I'll not be double-teamed. Now depending on how they take station as we approach I will pass larboard or starboard so I want you to have the guns loaded on both sides but not run out. Once we have decided I want you to keep up a rapid rate of fire. You may have to augment the gun crews from the opposite side to maintain the fire."

"Aye, captain," Dey replied. "We'll fire 'um till the barrels melt down."

Neptune tilted and Knight grabbed a rail to keep from losing his footing as the ship quickly came about. Taking his glass for a better look Knight realized just how right the lookout had been. She was a big un. The lead ship appeared to be a converted Indiaman. Forty guns at least and damn the lookout's eyes, he was right. The far ship was the *Barracuda*. *Well, Nancy*, Knight thought, *it could have been a wonderful life.*

BOOM! The forward ship, the Indiaman had fired.

"It'll be a costly affair sir." This from the master.

"Aye," Knight replied, "but you didn't expect to live forever did you?"

"Well, sir," the master replied, "I can truly say I'm right wid me maker but still while I'm ready I can't say as I'm raring to go."

Such wisdom, Knight thought.

Then Lieutenant Brooks was there, "It appears, sir, like that Dago can't stand not getting the first shot in, and he's overtaking the Indiaman."

Not believing his ears Knight picked up his glass to see for himself. Brooks was right. *Barracuda* was reaching on the lead ship and would pass to windward.

"That's it," Knight said. "They've made the first mistake. *Barracuda's* arrogant captain couldn't stand to let the Indiaman draw first blood. Hopefully, it'll be his undoing." Then Knight called to his master, "Set a course straight toward the bow of the Indiaman, then when I tell you veer to larboard. If all works well maybe we'll only face twenty guns on the first pass instead of forty or more."

"Aye," the master replied then ambled to the wheel.

Knight then called to the signal midshipman, "Mr. Byne, run up the signal, enemy in sight, then after a spell haul it down and acknowledge."

The mid looked dumbstruck at his captain, "Who are we signaling to, captain? The squadron is in Saint Augustine."

Knight snapped at the youth, "Damme sir, I know that but yonder ships don't."

Seeing the hurt look on the boy's face Knight relented, "My apology, sir. I'm in an ill mood and I've no right to take it out on you."

"Thank you, sir," the youth replied not believing the captain would apologize to the likes of him. "I understand now sir," the mid continued. "The signal is to keep 'em guessing."

"Right you are lad, now off with you."

BOOM!...BOOM!...

Fire from both ships now. The *Barracuda* had gained firing position.

"The next will be a hit if we maintain course, cap'n." This from the master, "If we loose our bowsprit we'll never be able to carry out your plan."

Knight who had once again taken up his glass spoke softly, "Patience, sir, patience."

Barracuda was to larboard but not yet along side the Indiaman.

BOOM!...BOOM!...

Both ships had fired again almost like they were in a contest. CRASH! A shudder went through *Neptune* as she took a hit forward. Almost like it was in slow motion. Knight could see bits and pieces of wood and splinters flying through the air. Looking forward the bowsprit and the bow chasers were intact.

"We lost part of *Neptune's* head, captain," Brooks volunteered speaking of the ship's figurehead.

"I believe we are almost in range now, Mr. Brooks. Have the gunner man the bow chasers and let those rogues feel *Neptune's* anger over being defaced."

"Aye, cap'n, we'll give a good accounting."

"Mr. Brooks."

"Sir."

"Have a care, should I fall, you will be in command."

"You'll not fall," Brooks replied as he went to carry out his captain's orders.

I wish I felt as sure, Knight thought.

BOOM!...BOOM!...

Again the enemy was firing. This time they fired high, trying to bring down the mast and riggings.

"Zur, zur," this was a petty officer. "Begging the cap'n pardon, zur, but the lookout 'as been calling to you, the Indiaman is full of sojars 'e says."

"Damme," Knight exclaimed, outgunned and doubly outmanned. The sound of cannons continued, both the enemy's and *Neptune*'s. The air was rent with the sounds of balls flying by. Then another crash forward and the hatch cover flew through the air.

Seeing it Knight looked to see if he'd given the order for the ship's boats to be set adrift. No need for them to add to the danger of flying splinters. Seeing they were gone he took up his glass again. Had he waited too long?

No, *Barracuda* was now directly along side of the Indiaman. She could never change course now without risking a collision. Then doubt came into Knight's mind. Was he falling into their plans? No...no...he'd not doubt himself.

Looking one last time he called to the master, "Now, sir, alter course to larboard and we'll pass the Indiaman and give her what for."

Then calling another midshipman, "My compliments to Mr. Dey, we will attack to starboard."

"Aye, captain," the excited youth replied then hurried off to deliver the captain's message.

It was too late now for *Barracuda* to change course. The broadside when it came seemed to vibrate the distance of *Neptune's* hull as the cannons went off almost in unison. They'd gotten the first broadside in but the Indiaman was returning fire, not with the precision of *Neptune,* but just as deadly.

Shudder after shudder as balls crashed into *Neptune's* hull. But Dey was as good as his word. *Neptune's* gunners were firing round after round. *Neptune* was fighting for her life and the gun crews knew it. Then they were past and the firing ceased, at least for the moment.

As the ship sailed out of the smoke that only seconds before had engulfed both ships the lookout called down, "*Barracuda* 'as tried to come about but now she's in stays, zur."

Hearing this, Knight ordered, "Put your helm down. Maybe we can get in a blow before she can recover from her confusion.

BOOM!...BOOM!...BOOM!...

Neptune let loose another broadside and Knight witnessed the accuracy of *Neptune's* gunners as ball after ball hit the *Barracuda.* But now the Spaniard was recovering and returning the fire. A scream forward as a ball plowed through and overturned a gun. A small explosion and then a fire. *They must have been reloading,* Knight thought. The fire was quickly put out by the gun crews to either side

Now *Barracuda* had completed coming about and was bearing down for the kill. *Neptune's* stern guns were firing now.

"Come about to larboard," Knight ordered. "Let's see if we can get the Indiaman between us again."

Then a loud crash from the stern and a runner reported, "Both stern guns 'as been 'it sir, all dead."

"Gunfire, sir, from out in the bay."

"Aye, Mr. Jackson, I heard it," Gabe answered. He too had heard the deep thud...and thunder of cannon fire.

"Looks like Captain Knight has met up with the rebel ship," Dagan volunteered.

"Ships, I'm thinking," Gabe replied, "I'm sure it's more than one from the sound of it."

The wind had picked up and on a full ebb tide Gabe was moving down the mouth of the river quickly...too quickly for the master.

"I know you want to help, sir," he said, "But if we run aground we'll be no good to anyone."

The master was right Gabe knew, but he couldn't bring himself to reduce sail, not with Knight taking on two ships. From the sound of it, big ships. Dagan glancing at Gabe seemed to read his thoughts, "I'll go aloft."

As Dagan ascended to the mainmast, Gunnells approached Gabe, "We're almost at the mouth of the river now."

Nodding, Gabe then called to the first lieutenant, "Mr. Jackson, beat to quarters. I want the guns double shotted and a measure of grape. We have to make a statement with our first broadside before they know we are alone."

"Aye, sir."

After what seemed an eternity but were only a few minutes Dagan was back at Gabe's side. "*Neptune* looks about done for. There's an Indiaman that's also in a bad way..." Dagan then paused before he continued, "The other ship looks like the *Barracuda*. She's got damage, but not so's she can't fight."

Jesus, Gabe thought, *what can SeaWolf do against such odds*.

"I'll not see Knight perish without trying to help," Gabe said.

"I never thought you would," Dagan replied as he put his hand on his nephew's shoulder, "but give a care, don't put yourself at risk." Then smiling he said, "Faith would never forgive me."

The cannon fire continued but it was now more sporadic. The lookout called down, "*Neptune* be playing cat and mouse wid de ghost ship, mostly keeping 'at udder ship between 'em bes' 'e can."

"Knight's a good captain," Jackson volunteered.

"I just hope we can save him," Gabe answered.

It was now less than two miles and Gabe could see the beating *Neptune* had taken. Even as he watched, *Barracuda* fired her cannons again and the proud *Neptune* gave a violent shudder.

"I can see boats in the water alongside the Indiaman," Gunnells said. He had been looking at the privateer while Gabe's attention was on *Neptune*.

"Well, maybe we won't have to fight both ships," Gabe said grimly. "Run up the flags if you will, Mr. Jackson. Mr. Lavery, I want every gun aimed and fired, I want every ball to hit home. Understand?"

"Aye, captain."

They were now in range and either they hadn't been seen or they were being ignored. *Some would call it suicide*, Gabe thought, *but even so he'd not turn his back on Knight and Neptune. Not while he had breath.*

The planks vibrated beneath Gabe's feet as *SeaWolf's* gun ports were opened and the guns rolled into firing position. *Lord, for what we are about to receive*, Gabe thought. Then as an afterthought, he prayed, *please be with Neptune's crew.*

A bareback seaman running by broke Gabe's reverie. Focus he said to himself, they were in such a position they'd face the *Barracuda* first, then....

The Indiaman was now obviously down in the water so unless her men boarded *Neptune* she should not be a factor.

"All ready, sir," Jackson reported.

"Very well, Mr. Gunnells. "We'll cross the Dago hawse and rake her as we go."

The distance was falling fast. *Should we take in another sail?* Gabe thought. *No, strike fast like Colonel Browne and his rangers are so apt to say.* Even though he was expecting it, Gabe felt himself jump as *SeaWolf's* guns went off, one after another her cannons fired. He was transfixed by the sight before him. The double shotted balls fired from *SeaWolf* crashed into the *Barracuda,* scoring hit after hit. He could see shrouds slashed, sails tore apart, and bright wood splinters flying through the air.

Lavery had the guns firing again as soon as they were loaded, reeking destruction with every ball. Smoke was now making it difficult to see but musket balls rained down from the larger ship and thudded into the deck. The whine of a ball made Gunnells wince as it flew past him striking the helmsman creating a third eye in the unlucky seaman's head.

They're not ignoring us now, Gabe thought.

Another man screamed as he was hurled to the deck by some unseen force, then blood gushed from his stomach spattering the man next to him.

"Keep moving," Dagan encouraged Gabe. "Otherwise, some marksman will be a guinea richer." In spite of the battle, the comment caused Gabe to grin.

The wind shifted and now the privateer was barely visible as it was engulfed in smoke. With visibility restricted on *Barracuda,* Gabe seized the opportunity.

"We'll go about, Mr. Jackson. Lay her on the starboard tack."

The wind was now steady from the south-southeast.

"Put the helm down if you please."

"Helm alee, sir," the new helmsman responded.

Jackson had the men working like demons on the sails.

"Man the braces. Heave…heave there you laggardly bugger," Graf shouted.

Around came *SeaWolf's* bow, yards groaning as canvas flapped, and then the sails snapped loudly as the wind refilled them.

Gabe then shouted, "Mr. Lavery, prepare to engage with the other battery, I want the guns firing no matter what. Fire as they bear."

Then as *SeaWolf's* guns fired and the smoke began to clear Dagan was again at Gabe's side. "They're quitting, look *Barracuda* has broken off."

"She's sailing away! David has once again defeated Goliath," Gunnells quipped. Relief was plain on his face.

"Do we give chase, sir?" Jackson asked.

"No," a relieved Gabe replied. "I don't know what we'd do if caught her. Unlike our master I don't believe we've defeated her. We've just wounded her and a wounded animal is frequently more dangerous."

As *SeaWolf* came about again Gabe peered at the once proud *Neptune*. Her stern had been blown open by *Barracuda's* heavy cannons. Her forward mast was gone, the mizzen mast was leaning. The deck gouged and splintered. To say she was badly mauled was an understatement.

Caleb had made his way on *SeaWolf's* deck, "We have two dead and only a handful of wounded."

"Good," Gabe said, "I'm thinking you'll be needed more on yonder hulk."

It's not good if you're one of the dead ones, Caleb thought, *but fate…er…Bart's lady luck was with them. Whoever heard of a brigantine attacking a large frigate anyway?*

As *SeaWolf* closed with *Neptune* a cheer went up. As Gabe, Dagan and Caleb went aboard *Neptune* the scene was horrifying. Men's faces were black with powder stains. Corpses littered the deck, great pools of drying blood was everywhere. One had to step over falling spars, rigging and ripped up planking. A few, under the supervision of the boson and the carpenter, were trying to set the ship back to rights.

"No holes below the water line," the carpenter said, "I'm not sure how long the mizzen will stand, not long if the wind gets up. The main mast appears untouched but we've no steerage. We'll have to be towed."

Looking about Gabe didn't see Knight or any of the officers. Dreading the answer he asked, "Did any of the officers survive?"

"Aye," the bosun answered, "the cap'n is hurt bad but is in his cabin, Mr. Dey is gone and they were taking off Mr. Brooks arm. The rest 'sides what you see," the bosun said, swinging his arm to emphasize the men on deck, "is dead."

"Caleb, would you be so kind as to check on Captain Knight?"

Without answering, Caleb made his way to the captain's cabin.

"Caleb has about had his fill of this sort of thing, I'm thinking," Dagan whispered.

"Well, so am I," Gabe responded, "So am I."

Chapter Twenty-One

It was a somber meeting when Gabe reported aboard the flagship. After he had finished his report Lord Anthony said, "I see you were able to salvage the Indiaman."

"Aye, sir, I sent Dagan and Lieutenant Lavery along with a boat crew over to search the vessel and Dagan returned saying that while the ship had been holed, very little damage was below the waterline. Lavery had already manned the pumps and was dumping debris over the side. Once we lightened her up a bit I felt she was seaworthy so we sailed her back."

"Were there any survivors?" Lord Anthony asked.

This brought a smile to Gabe's tired face. "I asked Lum that very question, sir. He had gone with the first boarding party and when I came aboard Lum was tossing bodies over the side. Any survivors I asked. He gave me a look of surprise and replied, 'You know Cap'n, Bart done told me you couldn't put no confidence in nuthin a Dago says, so I ain't ask if they's alive or not. I's jus' been dumping 'em over de side to help lighten da load like Mr. Lavery ordered."

This brought an appreciative smile to both Lord Anthony and Captain Buck.

"Gawd," Buck exclaimed. "I'm glad we don't have Bart and Lum together all the time."

The mood returned somber again when Lord Anthony asked, "Has Sir Raymond been taken to the hospital yet?"

"No sir," Gabe answered. "He's still aboard *SeaWolf* where we moved him before we towed *Neptune* back. Caleb said he's afraid to move him just yet. He had multiple wounds…gunshots and splinters. I waited as long as I felt wise before we started back, giving Caleb time to work on Captain Knight as well as the other wounded. *Neptune's* surgeon was lost at some point so Caleb had his hands full."

"What are Sir Raymond's chances of recovery?" Lord Anthony asked. "Did Caleb give you any hint?"

"No sir, he just said a lesser man would be dead. Lieutenant Brooks said that Captain Knight continued to fight the ship even after he'd been wounded several times. All the survivors on *Neptune* said Knight's ship handling is what saved them. He outmaneuvered those two ships time and time again so that until the very end only one of the enemy ships was able to fire on him at a time."

"And what of Neptune," Buck asked. "Is she seaworthy?"

Shaking his head, Gabe said, "I don't think so. Maybe if she was at some yard, but here…I think it unlikely."

"So," Lord Anthony said, "We've lost a nimble frigate and gained an old tub of a merchantman."

"Begging your pardon, sir, but the Indiaman is in overall good shape. The carpenters said she's well built…mostly of teak and she's sound. She's filthy and needs some repairs but I think she could be beached and put to rights here, sir. She's got forty guns, all new British pieces and she has lots of spare sails, ropes, cordage and even some spars in the hole. I put Lieutenant Jackson on board in charge of the prize crew and he said she handled well enough."

"Well, we'll see how repairs go," Lord Anthony said, not committing to any set course or plan. Then he spoke again, "I didn't see a name on her."

"No, sir," Gabe replied. "She had once been the *Lord Cromwell* but that's painted over. We were able to find some paper with the date of August 1775, so it appears the rebels took her about a year or so ago."

"What about the troops she was carrying?" Anthony asked, almost as an afterthought.

"I believe most made it to shore. Lavery did a quick count when he went aboard and said at least one hundred were dead."

"Damned, if Sir Raymond didn't make them pay dearly," Buck interjected.

"Aye," Gabe replied, "and we still don't know what damage *Barracuda* suffered. Something caused her to break off the action," he said. "I am sure it wasn't *SeaWolf's* pop guns."

"She may have believed the ruse with your flags," Buck said.

"Or perhaps like Sir Raymond," Lord Anthony added. "Her captain may have been wounded. Keep me posted on Sir Raymond's condition and when he can be moved ashore, Gabe."

"Aye sir."

Gabe sensed the interview was over. He was almost out of the admiral's cabin when Lord Anthony called, "If we salvage the Indiaman, what would you name her, Gabe?"

After a thoughtful second or so Gabe replied, "*Defiant.*"

"Why *Defiant?*" Lord Anthony queried. "Why that name?"

"Because the rebels took her, we took her back and now we defy them to try again."

"Good...very good. If you've no prior engagements sup with me tonight."

"My pleasure," Gabe replied. "I'll bring Lum and let him play you a tune on his fiddle. He is becoming very good with it."

"Good, see you then. Now, I must go fill in our Governor, else he'll send a messenger requesting my presence. He'll not be happy about those troops getting ashore."

Well, I could give a tinker's damn what he thinks, Gabe thought but kept his silence. *Politicians were quick to make war and quick to criticize but rarely did they have to suffer the hardships the fighting men did, be they soldier or sailor. Damme, I'll be glad when this war is over.*

The days and weeks that followed the battle with *Barracuda* were filled with monotonous patrols. Anthony had stretched his patrol area as far north as Charlestown and south to Havana. A few smaller privateers were taken but nothing was heard of the ghost ship. The Florida weather held true with hot days, frequent afternoon showers and warm humid nights.

The social activities paled in comparison to those experienced on Antigua. Still the governor had been gracious with invitations to Anthony's officers when an occasion did arise. Unlike the mostly British presence on Antigua, Saint Augustine was a very mixed bag culturally. Anthony had met a Minorcan priest, Father Pedro Camps, who was a very interesting man. He had started a book of records in which he kept births, deaths and marriages for the entire Minorcan community.

Anthony also met Reverend John Kennedy who was the schoolmaster of east Florida. He was a very educated man who never seemed to tire when talking of arithmetic, Latin or Greek. Anthony had allowed the good reverend aboard *Warrior* so that he might add a rudimentary knowledge of a sailor's life to his vast knowledge.

Of all of Saint Augustine's inhabitants, Anthony found he enjoyed spending time with some of the paroled prisoners of war the most. A few had their slaves with them and once their parole had been obtained, roamed freely about the city. Most of these were from Virginia, a few of which knew Dagan's Uncle Andre. Anthony spent many a night enjoying a good southern meal and listening to the talk of raising good Virginia tobacco and fine horses.

When not at sea Dagan spent considerable time with his uncle's friends learning more about the country where Andre chose to settle down. One night when Dagan and Lord Anthony were walking back to the waterfront Dagan remarked, "Is it not ironic that the people we enjoy the most are the ones we are at war with?"

Anthony nodded in agreement but his mind was on his wife and child, as of yet an unseen child. Sitting at the dinner table with the Colonial family and listening to the chatter had caused him to be morose.

Damn this war, he thought, *I wish it were over. Gabe could marry Faith and I could go be with my wife and daughter. But what of Dagan*, he suddenly thought. *What would become of him after the war was over? Would he want to move to Virginia to be close to his family or would he stay close to Gabe? What about Maria, Gabe's mother and Dagan's sister? Would she want to be with the family or stay in the house she'd shared with his and Gabe's father? So much that needed deciding*, he thought. *So much.*

Chapter Twenty-Two

Work had been started on the captured Indiaman to make her ready for sea and was now near being completed. Gabe had been right. Once cleaned up and repaired she proved to be a good ship. Without any official approval the men had taken to addressing the ship as *Defiant,* as Gabe had suggested.

Now that she was once again seaworthy Anthony faced another challenge. How to man her? Sir Raymond had improved enough to be moved from *SeaWolf* to the hospital at Saint Augustine but it would be a long time before he had recovered to the point he was fit for duty.

Anthony knew Stephen Earl was his only viable option to command her but whom would he put on *Merlin*: Earl's first lieutenant or Gabe? Gabe was ready for the next step up the ladder of promotion but then what about *SeaWolf*. Well, for now it was a moot point, because he didn't have enough crew to man the vessel, even with *Neptune's* crew available.

Thinking of this caused Anthony to think of the lieutenant's exam. Mainly it made him think of Mr. Davy. It was rare Gabe would approach him or try to influence him in anyway. But lately there had been hints dropped that Davy was ready to be made lieutenant.

"He's not yet eighteen," Anthony had argued.

"Neither were we," Gabe responded, "and he has twice the experience I had at that age."

"What about the six years aboard ship rule?" Anthony had mentioned. "Davy's only got four."

"That's just since *Drakkar*," Bart interjected, obviously an ally to the scheme. "Seems to me yew be's forgettin' them two years wot he was on board *Recourse*."

"He wasn't aboard *Recourse*," Anthony said somewhat sarcastically.

"See I tolds yew, yew be gettin' forgetful."

It was a common ploy to carry a name on the ship's books when the person had never set foot aboard in order to accumulate sea time, but to claim to be on board and your name not be on the rolls! Anthony had however relented ever so slightly as he did agree with Gabe and Bart. If anyone was ready for lieutenant it was Davy. Besides we're at war. Some consideration had to be allowed for this.

"Bring me his affidavits and if they look plausible I'll allow him to sit for the examination." Then looking at Gabe, Anthony said, "If anybody can round up a forged set of documents I guess Bart will know who he is."

Then without thinking Gabe said, "Bart and Gunnells already have them."

Seeing the look of disbelief on his brother's face Gabe made a hasty departure but not before Anthony had commented, "We'll all be on the beach if you two keep it up."

"Don't yew forget about Dagan," Bart said.

"Dagan, aye Dagan."

"See I told yew, yew be gettin' forgetful. Yew know iffen we's on the beach Dagan will be there with us."

"Damn your hide," Anthony bellowed but he was speaking to an empty doorway.

Davy and several other mids had passed the examination for lieutenant and now they were all at the Mermaid to celebrate. Now they couldn't wait for a billet to come open so they'd actually be commissioned. Buck and Earl had pulled Gabe and Markham aside and explained how hard they had drilled Davy. He did not get frustrated; he thought out his answers and did very well.

Then Buck said, "But anyone who could talk two King's officers into forging such a set of affidavits ought to be a lieutenant."

"Four," Markham said.

"Four, what do you mean four?" Buck questioned.

"I mean four officers. You two have known Davy as long as we have so you are as much a part of this as we are."

"Then it's five," Earl said. When the other three looked at him Earl continued, "Don't forget about his lordship."

"Humph," Buck said. "Best we be remembering. Gunnells signed his certificates and as one of the finest masters in the Royal Navy, I'd not question his word."

"Here, here," the group replied. "A toast to Gunnells."

As the merriment was winding down Domingo made his way over to Gabe. "To be a midshipman, is this something anybody can do?"

Amazed at his friend's inquiry Gabe said, "Yes. Generally there's a desire on behalf of the boy to have a life at sea. Then the father or guardian seeks a sponsor or perhaps they themselves will apply to a ship's captain for their son or someone they know to be favorably considered a midshipman. Most often if it's a relative of an admiral or person of influence; it's just being able to outfit the lad and provide him with enough of an allowance to live on. I must tell you Domingo that most midshipmen come from families with influence. A few such as Mr. Davy make lieutenant but without influence, to go beyond is almost unheard of."

"Do you think that I, as a humble merchant, would be able to outfit my son and provide enough allowance long enough so that he could decide if he truly wants to live a life at sea?"

Gabe was not sure how to respond. With what the tavern was now making, Domingo could outfit the boy, but with his Spanish heritage and no influence life would be rough. Even with his father being an admiral, it had been very tough for him at times. Gabe could only imagine how things would be for a Spanish tavern keeper's son in the Royal Navy. How did you explain to a 'landsman' what went on in the midshipmen's berth? How once signed on, the captain couldn't interfere least he is accused of favoritism. The lad would have to face up to bullies, poor food and a list of dangers that could take a life in a slip of a second. Not to mention the added dangers of war.

"Are you talking of Alejandro?" Gabe asked.

"Si."

"Has he ever been at sea?"

Domingo shook his head, "No."

"How is his education?" Gabe asked.

"It is well, señor. He speaks English and Latin and can do his arithmetic."

"Can he write well?" Gabe asked.

"Si, señor, he is very smart."

"How old is he?" Gabe asked.

"He is fourteen."

"Well," Gabe said. "He's older than I was and he's big and healthy enough to handle the rigors of shipboard life. Is he easy to anger?" Gabe asked.

To this Domingo raised his eyes and said, "Yes, sometimes too quick."

Well, thought Gabe, *what do I do?*

"Let me think on it Domingo and if I decide to take him on, I'll be his sponsor. That may prove helpful at some point."

As Gabe left the tavern he discussed the situation with Markham.

"I don't know," his friend said. "It would be a long shot at best. I'd talk to Dagan and see what he thinks. You know he's the one who'd know best except maybe his Lordship."

"Thanks," Gabe said, "for telling me what I already knew."

"Well there's no charge for the obvious," Markham quipped. "By the way have you seen Nancy lately?"

"Not that I can recall. Last time I saw her she was giving the nurses what for at the hospital for not taking proper care of Sir Raymond."

As the two friends walked on a thought came to Markham, "You know Gabe, Domingo is liable to lose both his children to the Navy: Nancy to Sir Raymond and Alejandro to *SeaWolf.* Bet he never expected that before we showed up."

The day dawned clear and warm with a humid breeze blowing across the anchorage toward the harbour. Gabe was hard to rise as was usual for him. He'd talked with Dagan and decided to allow Alejandro to come aboard for a trial. Dagan had felt it would be good for the boy to see another side of life, even if it was for just a short period.

Dagan had told Gabe, "If Domingo convinces some other captain to take the boy aboard, whether it is a merchant or naval vessel the chance of the boy coming home in less than a year would be doubtful. This way if in a few days he decides this is not what he wants, he can slip anchor and go ashore. If he takes to the sea you can sign him on."

Dagan had also recommended he spend some time with Davy while he was still a middy. "Let the two talk man to man so to speak," Dagan had said.

Gabe had sent word to Domingo for the boy to be ready this morning and Gabe would send for him.

"I'll go," Dagan had volunteered, "and on the way back we'll stop and visit on the *Swan* for a while. I'll see if Markham's anymore chipper in the morning than you."

"Take Lum with you," Gabe said. "We need several things for the pantry and have him check my store of cigars before he leaves."

"I'll tend to the tobacco," Dagan replied. "I'll get us some good hand-rolled Virginia leaf cigars."

Gabe hadn't missed the "us" in Dagan's comment. "You enjoy your evening visits with the Virginians I take it."

"Yes," was Dagan's only response.

"Gil tells me Colonel Manning's wife has a sister, a recently widowed sister. Does she add to the pleasure you enjoy during your visits?"

"She doesn't take away from it," Dagan replied matter-of-factly.

"Was I going to be told about this lady?" Gabe asked with a grin.

"It appears you've already been told."

"Is there a possible future relationship?" Gabe continued, realizing Dagan seemed a bit uncomfortable with the conversation.

"There's always a possible future," Dagan answered. "Now finish getting dressed and drink your coffee before it gets cold. Damned if you ain't worse at rising now than you used to be. All that hooting with the owls keeps you from soaring with the eagles."

Gabe had been working at his desk for the better part of the morning. Dagan had not returned so he was either still ashore or on *Swan*. The groan of a ship is something a sailor hears daily and learns to tune it out. However, the groans were becoming more frequent and the sounds of timbers creaking as waves were lapping at the side of the hull could be heard. As Gabe rose from his chair to go topside he could feel the slight heave of the deck as *SeaWolf* tugged at her mooring. A dark cloud blotted the sun from view and the sky had an ominous look.

Lieutenant Lavery was quickly at Gabe's side and said, "General signal from flag, sir, put to sea."

"Any sight of Dagan?" Gabe asked.

"Yes sir, he and a lad went aboard *Swan* about a quarter hour ago."

"Damn," Gabe swore.

The wind had picked up till it shook the shrouds. The normal greenish tint to the sea had now turned an angry blue.

Gunnells and Jackson were now present and the master declared, "We're in for a blow."

Taking a look toward *Swan,* Gabe still saw no sign of Dagan. "Damn," he swore again.

"Sir," this from Jackson, "*Merlin's* getting underway."

"Very well," Gabe replied. "Put to sea, Mr. Jackson. Let's see if we can outrun this tempest."

Then as the officer went about getting underway, Gabe took one last look toward *Swan*. *Where are you Dagan, where are you?* he wondered.

Chapter Twenty-Three

SeaWolf followed *Warrior* and *Merlin* out of the anchorage with *Swan* directly behind. The smaller *Rose* and *Audacity* would be safe inside the harbour. There'd not been time to do anything with *Defiant*, the captured Indiaman.

Just as *SeaWolf* got underway what felt like an endless gust of wind seemed to pick up the ship by the stern and drive her forward. Gabe ordered lifelines strung between the mast and ropes tied around the helmsman.

"Put two men on the wheel," Gabe ordered, "and have all the men not on watch go below."

The rain had now started and visibility had diminished. Gabe felt it better to have the men below out of the wind and rain until they were needed. He'd change the watch in two hours to keep the men fresh. Walking aft, Gabe had to time his steps to keep from loosing his footing due to the violent pitching and rolling of the ship. Once at the taffrail he raised his glass but was unable to find the *Swan*. *Did she take another tack?* he wondered.

The seas were rising and the wind now howled. Every wave seemed to be larger than the previous one with the waves pushing and lifting the stern so that the bow dipped down before the wave slipped from beneath the ship. The sea continued to grow and Gabe stared, fascinated by the phosphorescent water that gushed from the turbulent waves. The wind had risen until it cracked, groaned, roared and howled.

Gunnells approached Gabe wiping his eyes. There appeared to be no fear in the old master's face. "She's a fair tempest," he hollered trying to be heard above the wind, "but it ain't no hurricane. Running with the wind we should out sail this by dawn."

Looking at the enormous height of the waves Gabe hoped the master was right. He too had been in worse conditions, a hurricane in fact with winds over sixty knots. Still he was apprehensive, the morrow couldn't come quick enough for him.

The dawn came slowly as clouded skies still blocked the sun's rays. Throughout the night Gabe had stood with Gunnells keeping an eye on the wheel, the mast, the sails and the guns waiting for something to go wrong. It hadn't. Now the two were sleepy, hungry and near exhaustion.

"Could have been worse," Gunnells joked. "We could have been in the North Atlantic and we'd be near frozen."

Gabe was thankful they weren't. He was also thankful the master's predictions had come true and moderate weather had greeted the dawn.

Caleb came on deck and said, "Looks like it's clearing up."

"Aye," Gabe answered. "Many injuries?"

"Not unless you count Mr. Jewells."

"What happened to him?" Gabe asked.

"He fell when the ship took a roll and busted his lip on a bottle."

Gabe was afraid to ask a bottle of what.

Up forward a lookout called, "Sails fine on the larboard bow."

Jackson who'd gone below to get some coffee had returned on deck.

Seeing him Gabe ordered, "Send a man aloft now that the wind has moderated."

"Aye, sir."

Then taking his glass Gabe again looked aft but still no sign of the *Swan*. *Be with them God*, he silently prayed. Lum had come on deck and seeing the troubled look on Gabe's face tried to comfort him.

"They's be alright, cap'n. Dat Captain Markham is near bout as good a cap'n as you is and wid Mr. Dagan a heppin they's gonna be fine. Ain't no doubt in old Lum's mind. Shucks they problee already eating breakfast and wondering what's foh supper. Nah suh, don't you worry none. Da Lawd ain't gonna let nuthin' happen to 'em." Lum's ranting did make Gabe feel better.

"Mr. Jackson."

"Aye, sir."

"I think I'll go below and break my fast. Call me if any further sails are sighted."

"Aye, captain."

By noon the skies were clear and Lord Anthony's squadron of ships drove fast through the swells that only a few hours before had been a raging sea. The ships were on a nor'nor'easterly heading. Men were airing out their hammocks as the general signal to pass "make and mend" had been given throughout the squadron.

Gunnells being the old tarpaulin that he was had hinted to Gabe it wouldn't hurt to "slice the main brace" after the blow they'd been through. It was a common to allow an extra ration of grog after weathering a storm. It served as a good pick-me-up for the crew.

I should have thought of it Gabe realized but his mind was not on *SeaWolf* but on the ship he didn't see. He'd had a sinking feeling ever since they'd left Saint Augustine as the storm had blasted down.

"Maybe Markham had decided to make for the harbour," Jackson said.

"I don't think so," Gabe replied, "Markham would have tried to keep station on the flag."

Markham and Gabe had spent too many years together. First as midshipmen, then lieutenants; and finally commanding their own ships in the same squadron to not know how the other would think. No, Markham would not chance crossing a shallow bar to possibly find shelter in a harbour when he could put to sea and run as the squadron had done. No, wherever they were, they'd be together, Markham, Dagan and Davy. But not for a minute did Gabe think they'd be in port.

SeaWolf sailed to leeward of the flagship and the Florida coast was visible. It looked much more hospitable today than it did yesterday in the crashing surf and rain. *Was Dagan out there somewhere? If he was, he'd have Markham with him as well as Alejandro. Damn,* Gabe thought, *was the boy on the Swan? What kind of frightful experience was it for a boy to have to face a storm the first time he ever set foot on a ship? Well, if he survived and that didn't scare him away, nothing would.* Gabe instructed the lookouts to keep a sharp eye on the coast as well as the horizon. They may have run ashore.

The sun was like a fire in the sky and was starting to settle over the horizon. They were approaching the anchorage and Gabe's worst fears seem to be realized when the lookout called down, "There she be. There be the *Swan*, hove up on the island."

Snatching a glass from Jackson's hand, Gabe rapidly climbed up the shrouds and onto the lookout's platform. The lookout had been right. It was the *Swan*, her main mast was gone and she had been driven up and onto Anastasia Island. Several people were gathered around the wreck.

After Gabe made his way from aloft he returned the glass to the first lieutenant. "My apologies, Jem. I should have asked and not just taken your glass. It's *Swan* alright," he continued. She's been driven ashore and beat to a hopeless wreck. There are people gathered around her. I could make out Dagan but I didn't see Markham. If you will signal the flagship."

"Aye," Jackson replied, surprised at the apology and still more surprised at how much feeling and emotion his captain displayed. *Man has a heart*, Jackson said to himself. This was more evident when Gabe called to Lavery.

"Call Caleb, then man the gig and we'll go see about our friends." Then turning back to Jackson, Gabe ordered, "Take the ship to her anchorage unless otherwise ordered by the flag. I will be back directly."

"Aye, captain," was Jackson's only response.

Lord Anthony had read Markham's report and could find no fault with his actions. He would attach his findings and recommendations to Markham's report and hopefully the findings in regards to the loss of *HMS Swan* would go into some clerk's file never to be heard of again.

It was surprising how bad *Swan* was mauled and the Indiaman, Gabe's *Defiant*, had hardly been touched. However, he'd come to a decision and he'd put it into motion at dinner this evening. Buck, Earl, Gabe and Markham were to dine with him tonight and after the meal he'd unfold his plan. Silas walked out of the pantry in time to see the admiral smile. *Well smile, he should*, Silas thought, *and after the meeting tonight several others would be smiling and that's no error. Hopefully, Bart wouldn't let the cat out of the bag.*

It had been a fine meal and now cigars and pipes were being lit as the aroma of mixed tobacco filled the admiral's dining area. It was the first time since the storm that all the officers had gathered together. The only exception was Sir Raymond who was able to sit up now but was far from being fit for duty.

Markham was speaking of the dreadful day when the storm took *Swan*. "We'd just cleared the anchorage and was tacking astern of *SeaWolf* when a rogue wind of gale force almost broached the ship. The ship yawed to leeward and then there was a crack not unlike that of a cannon firing and the main mast went by the way. Mast spars, ropes and rigging all over the lee rail pulling us down into the sea. I sent men to clearing the rigging as the ship was listing badly starboard and in danger of being swamped."

Looking from the wine glass he'd been staring into as he spoke, Markham glanced at Gabe. "Had it not been for Dagan we'd have turned turtle and lost all aboard. However, Dagan had just cut through the last bit of rigging and the mast went over the side. Free from the weight of the downed mast, *Swan* righted herself only to be caught by a mountainous wave that lifted the ship like a piece of kindling and fairly drove us onto the island. Then if that wasn't enough, another wave not as big as the last but big enough seem to lift *Swan* then drop her on the huge stones tearing her bottom clean out. I could feel every crack of the timber like it was tearing my life clean out of my chest."

"However, after that last wave she was not touched again except by the fierceness of the wind and the blinding rain. It was too rough to venture off the ship so Dagan, the Spanish lad, Davy and I tried to keep dry and warm in my cabin and the crew stayed below in their berths. Towards dawn the winds died down and the rain stopped. It was then with the rising sun I realized my beautiful *Swan* was nothing but a battered hulk and she'd never see water beneath her keel again."

All was silent for a moment when Gabe spoke, "I recall the wind, Francis. It fairly slung *SeaWolf* forward. Had I been a minute longer getting underway I fear *SeaWolf* may have been setting alongside *Swan*."

Chapter Twenty-Four

Gentlemen," Lord Anthony was calling to the officers at the table. "We all share in Captain Markham's remorse but as with life, in death often a new life is born. I have spent the afternoon with the Governor and with his blessings I've decided to purchase the Indiaman…*Defiant*, for the Navy. You all understand that this has to be approved, but with both the Governor's and my recommendations I believe Lord Howe will agree. However, until he does the following changes are to be considered temporary. We all know the Admiralty Prize Court can be fickle at times."

This brought a chuckle from the group. Fickle was a mild way of putting it. Lazy and tight-fisted were better terms.

"Now then," Lord Anthony had began again, "I have asked Captain Buck to draft up a crew for the ship."

"Valley," Anthony called to his clerk, who'd been standing in the wings. "Valley here has a draft of assignments for each of you. Should anyone wish to change or swap a crew member you have but to log it in the ship's book. Now to specifics…Captain Earl, you are hereby given command of *Defiant*. Lieutenant Anthony, you are hereby temporarily, pending approval by Lord

Howe, promoted to captain and will assume command of *Merlin*. Lieutenant Markham, I have found no personal fault on your behalf in regards to *Swan's* loss. I have said as much in my reports. You are now to assume command of *SeaWolf*. I have left it up to each of you as whether you take your warrants or not. Make your desires known to Valley and he will draft up orders accordingly."

Glancing to his side, Lord Anthony could see the look of desire on Hazard's face. Well, empty sleeve or not he was a good seaman and a fine officer. As soon as available, he'd put him back to sea...on his own quarterdeck.

Since the storm a number of ships had gathered at Saint Augustine. More than at any time since the Royal Navy had established its presence.

"Looks like a sea of masts," Buck had commented.

Most of the ships were merchant ships from various nations. They had stopped to heal their wounds and make repairs needed after the recent storm. A few Navy ships had also stopped. The one that interested Lord Anthony the most was the mail packet. He longed to hear from his wife and find out how their daughter, Macayla Rose, was getting along. Caleb was quickly inquiring if Dagan had any news.

"No," Dagan replied then seeing the hurt in Caleb's face, put his hand on his friend's shoulder. "Caleb, there's nothing to keep you from going to visit."

After a thoughtful look Caleb said, "I am. I get the feeling we're not going to be here much longer but I feel I'll be needed before the squadron has new orders."

"Those are my feelings as well," Dagan replied. "It's a nagging feeling I've had for some time. I feel things are coming together that will put us in place to do battle with this *Barracuda*. It's then you'll be needed," Dagan said.

"Well, regardless if we do or don't," Caleb said, "Mr. Jewells and I are going to Virginia. You're welcome to come along, old friend."

"It's a thought," Dagan said, "even if for just a short visit."

Mermaid was crowded with all the ships in port. Gabe, Markham and Earl had just said their good-bys to Buck as he had an engagement for the evening.

"Leave it to Buck to find that one lonely lady in need of his time and talents," Earl joked.

"I hear Dagan has been spending time with the widow woman over with the Colonials," Markham added. "Is she going to be a widow much longer?"

"I've no idea," Gabe replied. "He's been closed mouth about their relationship. He did say they are going to be exchanged soon and will be headed back to Virginia."

More drinks were brought to the table and the subject changed to how fast things were going in regards to the new assignments. Earl had taken all his warrant officers to *Defiant* and Gabe had done likewise in transferring to *Merlin*. He'd kept Gunnells as master, Jackson as first lieutenant, Lavery as second lieutenant. The surviving fourth lieutenant from *Neptune* was now *Merlin's* third lieutenant and Mr. Davy now was commissioned and made fourth lieutenant. Midshipmen were scarce.

Governor Tonyn had put forth two boys and Reverend Kennedy had asked Lord Anthony to take two boys. Alejandro had decided to continue so they now had five new midshipmen. Lord Anthony had decided to partial out his three most senior mids so that each ship would have someone to help train the new lads.

Trying to find uniforms for those recently promoted had been difficult. Earl gave Gabe a spare captain's coat and Hazard had rounded up a lieutenant coat for Davy. Still everyone's wardrobe needed an overhaul but it'd have to wait.

As the evening wore on the group was finishing their final round when Domingo appeared at the table.

"Señor Gabe, would it be possible to speak to you of a private matter?"

The three just looked at one another sure this had something to do with Domingo's daughter, Nancy, and Sir Raymond. Earl and Markham downed their drinks and bid a hasty farewell.

"Cowards," Gabe hissed.

"Dagan is with Bart at a table by the door. I'll send him over," a smiling Markham replied to Gabe's remark. Markham did lean over to speak to Dagan who then made his way over to Gabe.

The two approached the bar where Domingo was turning the counter over to his wife. He beckoned to the two to follow him to a small storage shed behind the tavern. It was a small low roofed affair made of Coquina stone, which was hauled from Anastasia Island. Just inside the building, a smallish dark complexioned man sat at a table where a single candle gave forth a dim light. As the door opened the candle flame flickered creating little shadows that danced on the whitewashed walls inside the shed.

The table was small with only two chairs. A partial loaf of bread and a few crumbs of cheese were next to a half full bottle of Sangria. Fear filled the little man's eyes as Gabe and Dagan entered first, then relief when Domingo entered closing the door behind him.

"This is Paco," Domingo said by way of introduction. "He is my wife's cousin. He is a seaman." That much was obvious from the man's dress.

"Until recently he sailed on a ship out of Boston and was in charge of his captain's boat."

"A cox'n?" Dagan asked.

"Si, señor, a cox'n and how do you say it...a boatsman."

"A bosun," Gabe corrected.

"Aye," the little man said before Domingo could reply.

However, Domingo continued, "He was offered much to sign on to a privateer but he now thinks his captain is crazy so he...ah deserted his ship. He has come to me with much information and I tell him you are a fair man, Señor Gabe, and you can make a place for him on your ship. He thinks that is good...otherwise he feels his life is in danger."

"We can certainly discuss signing him on," Gabe replied. "What ship did he run from?"

"The ship you search for," the little man said, "the *Barracuda*. I have much information which I think will be useful to you."

Damme, Gabe thought, *we must have an interview with his lordship.*

"In the meantime let's keep...Paco, is it?"

"Si, Paco."

"Good. Let's keep Paco hidden so that *Barracuda's* spies don't find out about our friend being here."

As the captains settled into their seats in the admiral's cabin the atmosphere was much different. This was a conference for battle. A battle in which some of those gathered here today might not return. Heads went up as Hazard entered and held the door for the admiral.

"Well, gentlemen," Anthony said as he took his seat at the head of the table.

No pleasantries today, Gabe thought.

"It appears," Anthony continued speaking, "that lady luck has once again smiled down on us. We have reliable information that the *Barracuda* was just in an area some thirteen miles south of Savannah. This is a plantation owned by a fellow named Morel. Apparently there's a good landing area here and *Barracuda's* Captain de Lavago was treated for wounds he received in battle against Sir Raymond and Gabe."

"Our information is he has a vendetta against the British for the loss of his property. However, our informer tells us he is now a man gone mad by his hatred and worsened by his wounds. He recently flogged one of his officers to death over having to retreat from the recent battle with Gabe and Sir Raymond. He is now, I'm told, gone back to his lair, Cayo Hueso, or as some call it Key West. Because of the tricky currents and treacherous reefs on both sides of the channel this has been the perfect hideout. One we've thought about but not ventured into. But that's about to change. Our own Lieutenant Hazard knows these waters having participated in…ah…shall we say salvage operations there before the war."

This brought a chuckle from the group. It was known that the island had been a haven for wreckers at one point and the salvage for the most part was due to the wreckers luring unsuspecting ships onto the coral reefs.

"Now, we know de Lavago is a capable foe, madman or not. So we have to go about this boldly but with the idea of limiting our loss in case the plan doesn't work."

Hazard with the help of Bart had hung a large hand drawn chart of Cayo Hueso on the bulkhead.

"Lieutenant Hazard thinks *Merlin* and *SeaWolf* can enter the channel here. With only minimal room to maneuver he feels *Barracuda*, if she's there we'll up anchor and travel down the channel and out into open waters on the Gulf side. At this point he could come about and have a broadside waiting when the would-be chasers arrive. But that's not going to happen. We, that is *Warrior* and *Defiant*, will be waiting on him once he clears the channel. Now are there any questions?"

Markham was the first, "What if *Barracuda's* not there?"

Nodding his head, Anthony answered the question that was on everyone's mind. "The attack is to be a dawn attack. However, Lieutenant Hazard with a crew in a long boat will scout out the area before we proceed. We will lie off the coast until the reconnaissance is complete. If everything goes as planned this should be done by midnight which gives *Warrior* and *Defiant* time to sail around the Key and be in position by dawn."

"If he's not there?" Earl asked.

"I intend to set a trap not unlike the one he laid for *Pigeon*. The utmost in secrecy in regards to this plan cannot be expressed enough. Bart has already set out rumors we are going out on patrol, *Defiant* and *Merlin* to the north and *Warrior* and *SeaWolf* to the south. Let's hope it is believed."

"Boat ahoy!"

"*Merlin*."

The challenge and reply. Gabe had still not gotten use to the fact he now commanded...temporarily commanded, a frigate. Rated as a thirty-two gun ship her main battery consisted of twenty-six twelve pounders with two eighteen pounders on either side of the bow. Her secondary armament was four six pounders. *Merlin* was one hundred twenty feet long and thirty-four feet wide with a burden of about six hundred tons. Making his way down to his cabin Gabe found Dagan waiting.

"I'm going over to dine at Colonel Manning's. They are to be taken to Norfolk tomorrow and exchanged."

Gabe could tell Dagan was taking their leaving hard. "You've become quite close with the family haven't you, uncle," Gabe said using the name he'd used all his pre-Navy life.

"Aye," Dagan replied, the hint of a smile on his face at being addressed so.

"Go then, enjoy the evening…nay the entire night but one question before you go. What's her name?"

Before Gabe could blink Dagan's hand shot out and put Gabe in a headlock with one hand and tossed his hair with the other. Then just as quickly he was through the cabin door. Stopping suddenly he turned and said, "Betsy."

The marine sentry standing at the captain's cabin door, stood at attention, shocked at what he'd just witnessed. What a story he'd have for the mess that evening.

After a quiet meal Colonel Manning made his excuses about some last minute packing to do before they were ready to start their voyage home on the morrow. The servants set about cleaning and packing the dishes as Dagan and Betsy made their way to the swing on the front porch.

A faint breeze drifted in off the Atlantic and there was a quarter moon. Dagan was pleasantly surprised as Betsy nestled in beside him.

"I will miss you," Dagan said.

For a moment Betsy didn't say a word; then taking Dagan's hand said, "And I will miss you. I was a child bride, married at eighteen to the son of the man who owned the plantation next to the Colonel. He was rich, handsome, dashing and fearless and I thought I loved him. What girl wouldn't? He was made an officer in the Army of Virginia only to die of pneumonia before a shot was ever fired. But it's since I've been here...been with you that I really know what love is. I liked Thomas but I never loved him and I realize that now. But is it over before it begins?" She dabbed with her handkerchief at the tears starting to well up in her eyes.

Putting his arms around Betsy and drawing her close Dagan kissed at the moisture on her cheeks tasting the salty taste of tears. "No, my love, it's not over that much I promise you. You may have to wait but I'll come...I promise I'll come."

At that moment Dagan knew his words were true. His lips left her face and found her lips for a long, warm passionate kiss. She eased up onto his lap; their bodies crushed together, each feeling the other's heartbeat against their chest.

"My God, Dagan, I'm in love. I want you. I want you forever."

"Aye," Dagan barely whispered, "I want you and soon...soon mind you, you will be mine forever. You just wait."

"I will Dagan. I promise with all my heart...I'll wait."

Chapter Twenty-Five

Lord Anthony stood on the quarterdeck of *Warrior*. Small droplets of sweat dripped from his hair running down his neck to his back. Just out of sight of Saint Augustine they intended to come about and head southward. That is of course if no sails were sighted following them.

Buck made his way over and knowing his admiral as he did said, "Questions, doubts, always the what ifs. Don't you worry, my lord, we've covered every possible situation we could."

Nodding, Anthony replied, "You're right as usual, Rupert. Let me know when we sight the other ships."

"Aye, my lord."

As the admiral ducked into the companionway Bart winked at Captain Buck, "'E always worries but don't yew's fret. I's'll take care o' 'em proper like."

"Aye," Buck replied, "I'm counting on it."

Both knowing Lord Anthony's biggest worry lay in the fact that Gabe's *Merlin* would be the first to encounter *Barracuda* if in fact she lay in her lair as hoped for. Gabe was a seasoned officer and he'd handle himself well, Buck was sure but an extra prayer wouldn't be amiss.

It was just after midnight with a faint breeze blowing and a quarter moon shining down on the gentle ocean a mile off Cayo Hueso that *Merlin* picked up Lieutenant Hazard, Lieutenant Davy and the long boat crew. Once the longboat was brought aboard the orders were given to come about so they could rendezvous with the rest of the squadron who was hove to just out of sight of land.

"She's there," an excited Hazard had reported. "Not only is she there but from the number of campfires we spotted I'd say half the crew was ashore."

"We were close enough to hear their drunken laughter," Lieutenant Davy interjected, "as well as a few giggles from some of the little huts we could see that sat just at the shadows."

"Aye," Hazard confirmed, "and I'm betting there will be more than a few buggers hungover and nursing headaches in the morning from all the drinking and womanizing that seems to be going on."

"Any sign of her captain?" Gabe asked.

"No, we wouldn't know what he looked like of course but we didn't see anyone who was an obvious officer."

Once the rendezvous was made and Hazard's report relayed to Lord Anthony, final preparations were gone over and *Merlin,* with *SeaWolf* following, would enter the channel at first light. Once *Barracuda* was in range *Merlin* would start firing and if *SeaWolf* could bring her guns to bear she would concentrate her fire on the ship as well. If not, she was to fire on the batteries ashore or other targets of opportunity.

If *Barracuda* ran for it they'd be waiting and if she didn't an attempt to enter the channel would be made by *Defiant.* That failing a force would be sent in boats.

"She'll run," Paco volunteered. He had been brought forward due to his knowledge of the anchorage. "Capitaine de Lavago is not such a man to risk his ship or fight a battle without having the odds in his favor. He will run."

"Well, I damn well hope so," Buck had growled, ready to bring the rogue to an accounting.

Lord Anthony then asked the question no one else had, nor was it mentioned in the report by either Hazard or Davy, "Are there any other ships at anchor?"

Hazard's chin dropped and Davy suddenly looked crestfallen. Finally Hazard spoke, "We didn't see any others but a smaller ship could have been at anchor to the Gulf side of *Barracuda*. I didn't see any mast but as dark as it was I couldn't be certain. I'm sorry, my lord," a dejected Hazard said. "I saw the obvious and didn't try to get past the *Barracuda* to see if another ship lay alongside."

"No, you did the right thing," Anthony said wishing he had the information but trying to salve the young lieutenants sense of failure. *Damme, why hadn't he sent Bart or Dagan along. They would have looked then he'd know what lay ahead, not guess but know.*

Gabe straddled his legs and waited for the swell that caused *Merlin*'s bow to rise to glide past, then raised his glass to peer toward the small island or Key as Gunnells was so apt to correct. "Cayo Hueso is the Dago name. For us it's Key West," he'd say.

"Not yet light enough to see anything as of yet," Gabe said. He had come on deck at dawn as was his custom, shirt half buttoned, coat unbuttoned and hair all mussed.

"Good Lawd, sir," Lum declared. "One look 'et you'd plum scare dem pirates oudda dey skin. Better let Lum get you a comb."

"Later," growled Gabe. Sensing Gabe's mood Lum backed off.

"Good morning Mr. Jackson, Mr. Gunnells."

"Morning, captain."

The habitual greeting, the habitual reply.

"Mr. Jackson, let's get the men fed before we have to douse the galley fires."

"Aye, captain."

Dagan came forward with a cup of coffee. "Not like the kick you get with Silas's coffee but its got flavor," he said.

Silas always spiked his coffee wit a small tot o' sumthin' to get you going. Lum on the other hand added a small amount of chicory to his coffee that made the coffee strong but once the taste had been developed nothing else satisfied. Caleb had gotten to where he stopped by every morning for a cup and Dawkins wasn't shy about grabbing a cup, "to help me concentrate on me duties" he'd said.

It was now fast growing light and you could now see the Key in the distance.

"Let's get underway, Mr. Jackson…quietly if you will."

"Aye, captain."

"Mr. Gunnells, make our course sou'west by west."

"Aye, captain, sou'west by west."

"Deck there," the lookout called down, "Breakers on the larboard bow, sir."

"We've a good three miles," the master said without being asked as Gabe turned to him.

It was then that Hazard spoke, "Nothing to worry about, sir."

Gabe watched as the land became nearer. "Alter course two points to starboard, Mr. Gunnells."

"Aye, cap'n, two points it be."

"Damme," Gabe said, "I hate entering into a channel like this."

"I can get us through captain," Lieutenant Hazard declared.

Seeing the relaxed look on Hazard's face eased Gabe's anxiety somewhat but not completely. "Very well," Gabe replied. Then so that everyone on the quarterdeck could hear he said, "She's in your hands, Lieutenant Hazard."

"Aye, aye, sir."

Then to Gunnells, Hazard ordered, "We will alter course, steer west by north."

Then turning to Gabe, Hazard said, "I'd put a couple of leadsmen in the chain, sir."

Nodding to Graf, the bosun set about the order.

They were less than a mile from the entrance of the channel when Gabe ordered, "Clear for action, Mr. Jackson…quietly."

Quietly, aye," Jackson replied. He then asked, "Should we signal *SeaWolf*, sir?"

Somewhat taken aback by the question it took Gabe a moment to realize Markham was now on *SeaWolf*. He was on *Merlin*.

Feeling somewhat embarrassed at his momentary lapse he spoke sharply, "I assure you, Mr. Jackson, Captain Markham knows how to command his ship."

Gabe was instantly angry with himself and spoke again, "Forgive me, Jem, I had no call to speak that way."

"No apologies necessary, captain," the first lieutenant replied as he went about passing the word to clear for action…quietly.

"A touch of nerves?"

Gabe turned and was facing Caleb.

"We've not had much time to talk lately," Gabe said, feeling the need to talk to his friend.

"You've been busy," Caleb replied.

"Aye," Gabe answered, "but we should never get so caught up that we don't take the time to talk even if it's over coffee."

Then Caleb spoke the words Gabe knew was coming. "After this, when the time is right and things are settled I'm going to Virginia. I want to see Dagan's niece. I've a longing for her that will not go away."

Gabe had noticed the change in Caleb's demeanor around the wenches and thought so he's finally found the right woman. He could feel the emotion in his friend's voice but didn't trust himself to maintain his composure with the direction of the conversation so he jokingly said, "Are they ready for Mr. Jewells?"

The comment had the desired effect Gabe wanted and Caleb broke out laughing after a sudden look of concern. Men running to their battle stations broke up the conversation.

"We'll talk later," Caleb said.

"Aye, later."

As the men rushed about clearing for action Gabe felt like a bystander. He could hear the different sounds all mingled together as a sort of chaos became order, each man carrying out his assigned duty. The thud as screens were torn down, the sound of feet on the planks as seamen hurried across the deck, the clearing of hammocks and mess tables as they were cleared from the ropes and tackles of the guns.

The wisp of sand being strewn across the deck and rattle of metal as a tub of cutlasses was set, none too gently, on deck. Watching the scene, Gabe recalled Lord Anthony…Gil's quick words the brief moment they were alone before getting underway, *Have a care, Gabe, no heroics today…Gabe don't close with the ship, don't let them board you.*

Like quicksilver, the loving concern of a brother was gone, replaced by the duty of an admiral.

"Cleared for action, sir."

Damme, Gabe thought, *daydreaming again.*

"Very well," Gabe replied, joining Hazard and Gunnells by the wheel.

Only one helmsman had the wheel but another stood by, in case...in case. They were now entering the channel and the chance of danger increased with each passing minute.

Seeing Gabe's concern, Hazard volunteered, "She'll be fine."

Well, he may have traveled this channel many times, Gabe thought, *but not with some bloody rogue ready to blast you out of the water.*

Entering the channel you could see coral reefs to both larboard and starboard and there seemed to be a swirl of water indicating a change in the current. Looking over the side the water was crystal clear with multi-colored fish darting about in schools. A few jellyfish floated on the gentle swells and gulls hawked and hovered above, then like a flash dove after some tasty morsel.

Once inside the channel Dagan pointed out a pelican sitting on the stump of a dead tree. A crane standing in shallow water at the edge of a patch of twisted mangroves was startled by some unseen predator leapt up and flapped its huge wings becoming airborne while a white egret sat comfortably in her nest watching as they slipped past.

"It's hard to believe we're headed to a fight, doesn't it?" Dagan asked. "The place is so tranquil I hate to disturb it."

"Aye," Gabe replied. "I could get use to the lazy life on an island."

"Or a horse farm." Caleb had once again come on deck and spoke. This caused Dagan and Gabe to smile.

Seeing Davy approaching, Gabe turned his attention to his lieutenant. "Lookout says they can see *Barracuda's* mast, sir."

These were words Gabe had been expecting but dreaded to hear. "Very well, have our new midshipman, Mr. ...ah..."

"Hawks, sir. Richard Hawks," Davy reminded Gabe.

"Yes, well have Mr. Hawks signal *SeaWolf* enemy in sight."

"Aye, sir," Davy replied.

"Mr. Jackson."

"Aye, captain."

"You may run out the guns."

"Aye, aye sir."

Chapter Twenty-Six

The salt air had corroded the hinges on the gun ports so that they squeaked loudly as they were opened. A groaning sound emerged as men pulled on the ropes and tackles till the cannons were trundled into position and the word was passed by Lieutenant Lavery, "Guns run out, sir."

Gabe had ordered the guns be double shotted so the first broadside would be devastating. Not like *SeaWolf's* popguns, *Merlin* spoke with force.

Lieutenant Ferguson, the new lieutenant who had been one of *Neptune's* officers was forward by the bow chasers. He had an apprehensive look but Gabe thought who wouldn't after having been mauled as they had. This was his first action since that terrible day and if he didn't break today he'd be a fine officer.

Gabe forced himself to stand still while Lum handed him weapons, two pistols and his sword. Lum had a boarding pike and an axe while Dagan, true as always, had a blade the size of a claymore.

Gabe watched and as the bend was made shouted, "Fire, fire as you bear."

The hull seemed to jerk and shudder as gun by gun the double shotted cannons spit forth a flame of murderous hell. The charges ripped over the channel and into the unsuspecting enemy. As the guns were being reloaded Gabe could hear *SeaWolf's* guns going off as she concentrated her fire on the clearing beyond the *Barracuda*.

Gabe recognized the unmistakable sounds of grapeshot being fired from swivel guns. Then *Merlin* jerked again as her cannons slung the twelve balls crashing into the *Barracuda*. Hit after hit was scored as evidenced by debris flying through the air.

On shore screams and curses were heard. A few men and several half-naked women ran into the trees while others ran for their ship.

"No doubt about those whoresons having headaches now," Hazard said jubilantly.

Dagan was then at Gabe's side, "The look is calling down. There's another ship."

So there was cause for Gil's concern, Gabe thought. Looking beyond *Barracuda's* taller sides, sails could be seen as the smaller ship appeared to be headed out of the anchorage toward the Gulf. The ship had been sheltered from the onslaught by the bigger *Barracuda*.

Gabe had ordered all sails reduced before entering the channel but *Merlin* seemed to be gliding along faster than he wanted. He was about to reduce more sails when a hurrying Jackson skidded to a halt almost touching Gabe.

Shouting to make himself heard he said, "*Barracuda's* slipped her anchor cable and her bow is coming around."

How? Gabe thought. Then it suddenly came to him. While de Lavago may have been surprised he'd kept his wits about him. Now with a glass Gabe could see *Barracuda* turning. They had passed a towline and the smaller ship was towing the larger ship down the channel.

Still looking through his glass, Gabe saw *Barracuda's* gunports open as she was pulled so that her guns came to bear.

"Down," Gabe cried. "Everyone down."

No sooner had the words been shouted than the air was rent with a flaming hell. It was like a volcano erupted as cries and screams mixed with the sound of shattered rails and torn planking emerged in to one.

Thank God SeaWolf was astern, Gabe thought, as he lifted himself up from the torn deck. *Damn that cunning bastard, de Lavago*, he thought. *He'd one chance and he'd taken full advantage of it. Thank God, bow's on as they had only had a third or so of the cannons found their mark. That was bad enough*, Gabe thought, as some men were being carried down to the surgeon while others, no longer recognizable as a man were being unceremoniously dumped over the side.

Seeing the bow chasers were still intact Gabe called, "Lieutenant Ferguson."

"'E's done fer, sir," A gun captain said. "The *'Cuda's* done got 'em."

I didn't even know the man, Gabe thought, *but he seemed to know the…how did the gun captain say it…the 'Cuda. The 'Cuda had his number*.

Turning his attention to the gun captains of the bow chasers, Gabe said, "An extra tot to the first crew to put a ball up…*'Cuda's* arse."

This brought a cheer as the two crews raced to get off the first shot. Just before the guns went off Gabe heard a crashing sound as *Merlin* gave a shudder.

"Damme," he shouted. "Where'd that come from?"

"They've a battery ashore," Lieutenant Davy volunteered. "I saw the smoke from the mangroves yonder."

"Get this wreckage cleared," Gabe ordered.

Another crashing sound and Gabe raised his glass to see if there was enough smoke to pinpoint the battery. "Mr. Lavery."

"Aye, captain,"

"I want you to lay a barrage on yonder mangroves. There's at least two guns in there. Twenty-four pounders at least from the sound of them."

"Aye, aye captain."

Men were running in confusion as another ball scored a hit on one of the gun crews.

"God be merciful," Gabe whispered in a swift prayer. He was suddenly pushed backwards as a falling spar impacted with the deck creating a jolt throughout his body. Men were all about hacking away at the ropes and lines attached to the spar then when cut free dumped over the side.

A loud bang from forward attracted Gabe's attention as a cheer went up from the larboard bow chaser.

"Up 'is arse it be," the gun captain cried.

Then a loud boom ashore, *Merlin's* gunners must have hit the powder store for the shore battery as flames gushed into the air.

"That'll do them buggers," Gunnells declared.

There was no longer any fire from ashore so Gabe ordered, "Cease fire, cease fire. Mr. Lavery."

"Aye, captain."

"Mr. Druett."

"Aye, captain," the gunner replied.

"Keep a steady fire going with the bow chasers. Maybe we'll get lucky and give the '*Cuda* a taste o' what we gave the rogues ashore."

Lord Anthony walked the deck of *Warrior* unable to relax. It was already 'hot' in his cabin and only slightly better topside where a zephyr teased, disappeared then returned. It was now past dawn and impatiently he waited.

Warrior and *Defiant* had been at anchor for over an hour now. Glancing at Buck, the flag captain shook his head, "Nothing to report, my lord."

Bart appeared to be just as miserable himself only he'd had the good sense to remove his coat, so at least the heat was more bearable. Anthony had refused to remove his, citing the need to be recognized by the crew.

Bart had snorted, "'Em wot don't recognize yew now never will no matter wot yews wear."

As the dawn broke Anthony could smell the aroma of pipe tobacco drifting across the deck. Bart had waited till the glow of the match wouldn't be seen ashore then lit up. His way of dealing with the stress of waiting. Silas had just brought him a glass of lime juice when he heard a distant rumble, not unlike thunder just over the horizon.

He walked to the lee rail and was met by Bart and Buck who drawled, "Gunfire by Gawd. Gabe has come to grips with the cutthroats."

Now the sound had become distinctive as the deep percussion of *Merlin's* cannons was followed by the bangs from *SeaWolf's* six pounders.

"Damme, if they ain't pouring it on," Buck said proudly.

"Hopefully they are giving and not receiving," Anthony said with a concerned voice.

The sound of gunfire continued almost in a rhythm when suddenly the unmistakable sound of a heavy broadside filled the air.

"That wasn't Gabe," Buck exclaimed.

Biting off a bitter retort Anthony tried to control his emotions as he felt his chest heave and a sickening wave of nausea swept over him. He gripped the bulwark trying not to be sick when Bart got his attention.

"*Merlin* be firing again, Gabe's giving the sodomite wot for again."

Anthony's ears now picked up what Bart's keen hearing already had. *Thank God*, he thought.

"Deck there," a cry from the lookout, "Two ships coming out 'o the channel. One be a sloop hit be. Tothers a frigate."

"'Bout time the bastard taste some real metal," Buck declared.

"I agree," Anthony said. "You may fire when convenient, Captain Buck, and pass the word to *Defiant* to do likewise."

"Aye, my lord."

"Rupert."

"Aye, sir."

"Concentrate on *Barracuda*. No prizes today. I want her sunk."

Buck was taken aback by the vehemence in Anthony's words but understood. They'd lost too much to this ship. "Sunk she'll be, my Lord, she'll never taste wind in her sail again."

Warrior had cleared for action at dawn and men rested beside the guns. "Now," Buck ordered, "open gun ports, run out, fire, fire as you bear."

The combined broadsides of *Warrior* and *Defiant* struck the unsuspecting ship a devastating blow.

"It was like she had ran aground when the first balls hit," Bart said, "She'll not last…she be sunk and jus don't know it…yet."

Yet defiantly the *Barracuda* turned directly toward the Anthony's two anchored ships. A shout from above as the lookout called down, "*Merlin's* clearing the channel."

A sense of relief came over Anthony. "Captain Buck."

"Aye, my lord."

"Signal *Merlin* to give chase to the sloop."

"Aye, my lord."

"Look yonder, sir," this from Herrod, Buck's first lieutenant. Fire was amidship of the *Barracuda*.

"He's turned her into a fire ship by Gawd," Buck swore.

However it was obvious the ship was well down in the water and with the next broadside she broke in half and sunk immediately. There had been a steady stream of sailors jumping clear as *Barracuda* was being pounded by Anthony's ships.

Buck turned to Lamb, his second lieutenant, and said, "Put someone in the boats and pick up any survivors." Then as an afterthought he looked toward Anthony, who nodded his consent.

"Deck there," the lookout called again. "*SeaWolf*'as cleared the channel."

Anthony breathed another sigh of relief. "Captain Buck, signal *SeaWolf* to assist in giving chase to yonder sloop."

"Aye, my lord, but I doubt Gabe will need any assistance."

Turning their attention to *Merlin*, Anthony could see Gabe had just fired a warning shot across the ship's bow. When the warning was ignored Gabe fired a broadside. This took down the forward mast which half hung over the side creating the effect of a sea anchor. This did it. As the ship carried no flag, the captain had the bow put into the wind and the sails hauled down.

"'E struck," Bart declared.

Gabe, Dagan, and Gabe's new cox'n Paco filled the captain's gig with a crew while Lieutenant Davy and a squad of marines under Sergeant Schniedermire pulled toward the sloop.

"Look," Gabe called to Dagan. "No wonder she got away so easy. She's been pierced for sweeps."

"Aye," Dagan replied. "They pulled themselves around without us being any wiser and only set sail when they were ready."

Hearing the conversation Davy couldn't help but feel a bit of guilt. He'd wanted a better look but hadn't insisted. If *Warrior* hadn't been lying in wait *Barracuda* would have gotten away.

"Lieutenant Davy."

"Aye, captain."

"Have the marines board from the starboard while we board from the larboard side."

"Aye, captain."

"Mr. Davy."

"Aye, sir."

"Keep a sharp lookout. I don't trust these rogues."

"Aye, aye sir."

One of the sailors forward used a boathook to grab onto the chains. As per custom Gabe stood up in the stern sheets only to be surprised when Dagan climbed up the tumblehome and through the port. This had taken the crew totally off guard but all eyes remained forward and nobody spoke. With a quick breath Gabe reached out and hauled himself out of the boat and through the entry port.

Once on deck, Gabe could see the marines were formed up and ready to fire. Behind him the gig's crew boarded and fanned out. The sloop's crew was gathered between the main mast and the quarterdeck.

Dagan was there and as Gabe drew abreast he whispered, "Careful now, I've a feeling."

This explained his actions in departing the gig. Gabe quickly noted the flushed deck and sixteen twelve pounders and it reminded him of *SeaWolf* but more like a small frigate.

This will make a nice prize, he thought. Taking a few steps toward the sloop's crew he said, "I'm Captain Gabriel Anthony of *HMS Merlin*. You have been taken and are now my prisoners. May I ask which of you is in command?"

The sailors before him were a mixed lot, Spanish, Negro's and a few British. They were dressed in slops, most were barefoot and all looked defeated.

"I ask you again," Gabe said, his voice now raised. "Which of you is in command?"

When no one spoke Gabe called, "Lieutenant Davy."

"Aye, sir."

"Line the prisoners up into two columns and have each man searched. Then have the ship searched."

Then turning to the marines he said, "Sergeant Schniedermire, shoot the first man who makes a false move."

"Aye, captain. Marines take aim and if a man so much as moves a hair sideways pluck it for him." The harsh brogue voice of the marine sergeant seemed to leave little doubt in his willingness to cut a man down.

Turning aft Gabe called to Dagan and Paco to assist him as he searched the captain's cabin. At that time a scream pierced the air and a dark figure jumped from the companionway, a sword in one hand and a pistol in the other. He charged screaming curses toward Gabe, his gaunt face emblazed in hate and fury.

Gabe knew he was dead but suddenly Dagan shouted, "deLavago halt."

Almost like magic the man slid to a halt not three paces from Gabe. *So Dagan was right*, Gabe thought. *The rogue hadn't gone down with his ship. He'd bet we would let the sloop go to capture Barracuda only he hadn't counted on Warrior and Defiant lying in wait.*

Again Dagan spoke firmly, "It's over."

The half-crazed man took a deep breath and seemed to sigh. The contorted face seemed to relax and tears poured from his eyes and down his face. Then very deliberately he cocked his pistol and stuck the barrel to his chin and pulled the trigger. A sudden silence followed the bang.

All stood in awe at what they had just witnessed. No one was able to speak as they stared at the man slumped in a pile on the deck. Without understanding why, Gabe removed his coat and placed it over the fallen man.

Hearing steps across the deck Gabe saw Dagan headed toward the entry port and the gig below. Once again Dagan…his uncle…his protector had saved his life.

Gabe still felt numb as he said, "Lieutenant Davy, the prize is yours. I'll send a prize crew over. When you are ready to get underway make a signal and take station on *Merlin*."

Lieutenant Davy was also dumbfounded at the scene which had just taken place. Even more so when Gabe…the captain had said the prize was his. Well he'd make the captain proud. There'd be no more errors if Lieutenant David Davy could help it.

As the crew pulled back to *Merlin* the rhythm of the oars was almost hypnotic. Gabe couldn't help but wonder if things had been different; *if Spain had kept Florida and England had kept Havana. Would he be here today? Would Don Luis de Lavago be lying on a ship's deck dead from his own hand or would he be sitting on the veranda of his plantation drinking a glass of wine and smoking a cigar. What about de Lavago's family? Did England or Spain care what their actions had set forth? The destruction of a man. The destruction of his family. Damn all politicians*, Gabe thought.

Epilogue

Lord Howe's flagship was at anchor when Lord Anthony's squadron returned with the sloop, *Ram*, as a prize. Lord Howe was ashore but a messenger from the Governor arrived on board almost before *Warrior's* anchor was dropped. Governor Tonyn was having a reception for Lord Howe and Lord Anthony and his captains were invited.

The reception that evening proved to be more spectacular than Anthony would have imagined based on previous events. He was shocked when a Negro footman with a white powdered wig took his hat and announced Admiral Lord Gilbert Anthony. The ballroom seemed to be teeming with people, all smiles and politeness. A momentary pause as Anthony was announced then the conversations renewed.

What a farce, Anthony thought. The Army's scarlet coats were everywhere and Anthony quickly spotted Provost in conversation with Governor Tonyn and Lord Howe. A few marine officers were present as was one or two of Browne's ranger officers. Anthony was amazed there were so many civilians. They'd not been many at other receptions.

Bare shouldered ladies flashed their fans and Anthony was amazed at the amount of bosoms being paraded. He then recalled Lady Deborah's words, "look, don't ogle." Well he'd have to pass the word to Buck who was definitely ogling. *I wonder if she's the one who Buck's been keeping company with?*

Feeling a hand on his shoulder Anthony turned to be greeted by Colonel Browne. Seeing where Anthony's gaze had been, Browne said, "With all these beautiful ladies it makes you wonder why a man would leave his home and bed to go fight a war."

"Aye," Anthony replied. He couldn't disagree.

Anthony waited until Provost had made his way toward a servant to get a glass of wine then approached Howe, "My Lord."

"Ah…Lord Anthony. My flag captain tells me a celebration is in order. I understand you've sank the privateers who's been reeking havoc on our convoys and got a nice little prize to boot."

"Aye, my lord," Anthony replied. "Good fortune was with us."

"Good," Lord Howe said. "We will talk later, on the morrow after I've read your reports. Now Governor Tonyn tells me it's time to dine."

Taking their places at the huge table Anthony saw no expense had been spared for Lord Howe's reception. He could almost imagine the tables groaning under the weight of so much food. Footmen and servants were everywhere, pouring wine; removing dishes as delicacies of every kind were being served; various tempting fruits and pies, meats, potatoes, carrots and breads. *How could so much food be consumed in one evening?* Anthony wondered. There was enough here to feed his squadron for a week.

There were silver punch bowls filled with Tonyn's favorite wine, Sangria, and even that had slices of oranges floating on top along with small remnants of ice used to cool the wine. Recalling Bart's words that he'd taken on a portly appearance, Anthony vowed he'd eat lightly. And he did until the desserts were served. Seeing the orange sherbet, fruit pastries, apple tarts and various puddings the vow was forgotten.

The shrill of pipes were barely out of Anthony's ears when Lord Howe's flag lieutenant greeted him. *I'll bet the flag captain is still abed with some obliging woman*, Anthony thought. He then introduced his flag lieutenant to Lord Howe's.

Anthony and Hazard were escorted to Lord Howe's waiting area and the flag lieutenant took Anthony's reports to the admiral. Feeling the after effects of last evening's reception, conversation was minimal. Hazard was thinking of the privileges that had come with being Anthony's flag lieutenant. Experiences he'd not encountered before nor would he again unless by some miracle he made admiral.

He was also grateful at the trust that had been given to him to pilot *Merlin* through the channel at Cayo Hueso. He'd attempted to voice his appreciation but was cut short by Howe's flag lieutenant telling Anthony that his lordship was ready for him.

"Take a seat, Gil," Lord Howe said, creating an informal environment. This meant his lordship was pleased. "Governor Tonyn has spoken very highly of you," Howe started, "You've greatly improved the Navy's reputation after the blunders of your predecessor."

Anthony noticed Howe disdained even to speak Sir Percival's name."

"How is Sir Raymond?" Howe asked.

"He visited the flagship this morning, my lord. He appears to be progressing well. I'm sure he'll be fit for duty soon. He's to be married soon. His visit this morning was to extend invitations to the wedding."

"Speaking of weddings, how is Lady Deborah?" Howe asked.

"She is fine and we now have a daughter."

"Well congratulations," Howe said.

He and Anthony had been sipping on lime juice so he raised his glass, "To mothers and daughters."

After the toast, Lord Howe picked up a paper he'd been taking notes on, "Gil, since you came out from England in 1775 you've patrolled the West Indies, the American coast from the Keys to Maine and you've also patrolled the waters of Nova Scotia. You've prevented an invasion, and you've taken some twenty-seven prizes including the sloop you've just brought in. I lost count of the enemy ships you've sank and prisoners you've taken. Because you've been so successful I've approved Gabe's captaincy as a testament of gratitude for your ceaseless service and success."

"Some will be jealous of the boy making captain, be prepared. He's earned it and I know you would not have recommended him if he'd not the experience to support it. However, some will see it as nepotism. Now do you have a deserving officer for this sloop you've just taken?"

Anthony thought of Hazard but said, "Captain Buck's first lieutenant, Mr. Herrod, is who I'd appoint, sir."

"Very well, I'll draw up the papers. *Defiant*," Howe said. "Is she seaworthy?"

"Aye, my lord. She is as fine a ship as we could hope for."

"And Captain Earl?" Howe continued his question. "Is he ready to hold permanent command of a forty gun ship?"

Once again, Anthony answered positively, "He has been with me almost as long as Buck has. I have the utmost of faith and trust in him."

"Very well," Howe replied. "I will confirm his appointment and I've already agreed to purchase *Defiant*. Now Lord Anthony, as to yourself. It grieves me to tell you this but you are being sent back to England."

"The entire squadron, sir?" Anthony asked.

"Yes…no, not *Defiant*. She will remain here at Saint Augustine with the sloop and the little island schooner. After your success I doubt we'll have to worry much about privateers. Now go home. Your tour has made you a rich man. Spend it on Lady Deborah and the little one. I've no doubt you'll be hoisting your flag again soon so enjoy your time."

Then Lord Howe exhaled deeply, "I wish it were me going home."

All of Lord Anthony's officers including Sir Raymond were gathered in his dining area aboard *Warrior*.

"Gentlemen," Anthony spoke. "I've important information from our commander in chief. *Defiant* and the sloop, *Ram*, are to be purchased. Captain Earl, you have been confirmed to command *Defiant* and you will receive orders directly. Lieutenant Herrod, you upon Captain Buck's recommendations have been given command of the sloop, *Ram*, and are promoted to the rank of Master and Commander."

A chorus of cheers broke out.

"Commander Herrod, you will receive your orders along with Captain Earl. Gabe…Captain Anthony, Lord Howe has approved your promotion and command of *Merlin*."

"Now gentlemen, with the exception of Captain Earl's *Defiant* and Herrod's *Ram* the squadron is to return to England."

As the cheers quieted down Buck asked, "When do we sail?"

"Lord Howe has given me a bit of latitude here," Anthony replied, "but I think by the end of the month at the latest."

After the meeting broke up Anthony spoke to Gabe as he was leaving, "Dine with me tonight and bring Caleb, Dagan and Lum."

Later that night after a filling but simple meal, Anthony, Gabe, Hazard, Bart, Dagan and Caleb sat back smoking their pipes and cigars as Lum played tunes on the lotz and then the fiddle.

As Lum played Dagan announced, "Caleb and I are going to visit Virginia."

"Aye, I've been thinking the wind blew that way," Anthony said with a smile on his face. Then turning to Gabe he continued, "I'd not take it amiss if you were to slip into Savannah and pick up a passenger for the trip to England either."

Now Gabe was all smiles. Overhead the ship's bell rang.

"I 'ears bells a ringin'," Bart said, "And soon hit'll be wedding bells I'm a thinkin'."

Appendix

Historical Note

In 1763, the Seven Years' War, or as it was called in America, the French and Indian War came to an end. Great Britain and her American colonies had won against the combined forces of France and Spain. The armies of Great Britain had conquered Canada and several French-held islands in the Caribbean. They had also stormed and occupied Havana, Cuba, Spain's principal seaport and administrative headquarters for much of Spanish America. In 1763 a treaty of peace was signed that left Canada to the English, returned several Caribbean islands to the French, and provided for Havana to become Spanish again in exchange for the province of Florida. Great Britain now controlled all of North America east of the Mississippi River.

When Florida was officially transferred to the English, most of the Spanish residents chose to depart for Cuba. Some stayed, especially the very poor, many blacks, and individuals of mixed blood. Even a few of the wealthier Spanish settlers remained to maintain their extensive properties and investments in Florida. At least one stayed to spy on the English.

The English had obtained a great continental peninsula with its eastern boundaries on the Atlantic Ocean, and its western boundaries on the Mississippi River. As the Spanish had done, they divided the new province into two parts. All the lands west of the Apalachiola River, including the very small settlement at Pensacola, became British West Florida and a part of the

history of this region. The eastern lands, basically the
Florida peninsula itself, became British East Florida,
headquartered in Saint Augustine, home for virtually all
of Florida's residents.

In 1775, when armed conflict commenced, British
East Florida's security rested on the rather inadequate
shoulders of a few companies of the English 14th and 16th
Regiments of Foot and a handful of artillerymen at the
Saint Augustine fort. By October of 1775, drafts of
troops sent north had reduced the regular garrison in
Saint Augustine to thirty-five soldiers of the 16th Foot
and a company of hastily raised and ill-trained local
militiamen. In the months that followed, Florida's new
governor, Patrick Tonyn, directed a number of small
blockhouse forts to be constructed to help protect the
province. Forts were established at Picolata, Anastasia,
Matanzas, and Smyrna. A more substantial structure,
Fort Tonyn, was built where the King's Road from Saint
Augustine crossed the St. Mary's River, the official
border separating the colonies of Georgia and Florida.

The Rebels to the north considered Florida to be a
natural, or at least, a very desirable, part of the soon-to-
be-declared new American nation. Their first act of war
in Florida was the seizure of an English brig, the *Betsey*,
and its load of 111 barrels of gunpowder by a Carolina
privateer ship within sight of Saint Augustine. Between
fall of 1775 and early spring of 1776, the Rebels raided
Loyalist settlements along the Georgia-Florida border.
With fewer than four hundred muskets within its
borders, Florida was virtually defenseless by land. Only
the sloops, and later, frigates of the Royal Navy
protected Florida from seaborne invasion. This essential
function of the Navy would continue and prove crucial
to the ultimate survival of British East Florida in the
violent years ahead.

In the early summer of 1776, the American Rebels assembled a force of more than two thousand men in Savannah, Georgia, under the command of Colonel William Moultrie. The mission of this force was to invade and conquer Florida. Fortunately for Florida, command problems and widespread sickness so crippled this small army that it never advanced farther than Sunbury, Georgia. Even had it actually invaded, Florida was no longer quite as defenseless as it had been a few months earlier. The first contingent of the King's 60th Regiment of Foot (Royal Americans) had arrived in Saint Augustine under the command of Colonel, later Brigadier General, Augustine Prevost.

As important to the future survival of British Florida as the arrival of the 60th Foot, was the arrival of Thomas Browne, formerly of Augusta, Georgia. A man of quite considerable competence and energy, Browne had been tarred, feathered, and partially scalped by Georgia Rebels for his loyalty to King George III. Recognizing his merits, Governor Tonyn commissioned Browne a colonel, and authorized him to raise, equip, and lead a force of irregular militia. This force would be called the East Florida Rangers. Rarely numbering more than two hundred, Browne and his Rangers assisted by a large band of partially red-coated Seminole Indians, were to perform signal services to the crown during the next few years.

American privateers roamed the Atlantic Coast from Canada to the Caribbean Sea, capturing enemy merchant vessels and effectively blockading the east coast of Florida, the Tory residents (British) of Cow Ford (Jacksonville) were unable to obtain supplies and so fled northward into Bullock County, Georgia.

Following this incident, the British Navy would successfully patrol the ocean, intercostal waters, and rivers.

On November 2, 1775 Governor Tonyn issued a proclamation that invited the loyalist to come to Florida and promising them free land. Starting in the spring of 1778 large groups of Loyalist exiles from South Carolina arrived in Florida. The men formed two small regiments—the South Carolina Royalists and the Royal North Carolina Regiment. Other men enlisted in Browne's Rangers.

In the fall of 1776 the first batch of prisoners arrived in Saint Augustine from Virginia. There were twenty-eight prisoners and their slaves sent by Lord Dunmore. Some were kept on the sloop, *Otter* that was used as a prison ship. Some including Colonel Lawson and Captain Weltcoat were kept in the fort.

In 1780 the brig *Bellona* under Captain Harrison from North Carolina drifted on to Anastasia Island. The crew of seventy plus men was made prisoners by the guards in the lighthouse. Some were held there and some were taken to the fort. Some of the European captives entered the 60th Regiment and some joined the British Navy.

Some French were also held prisoners here. They included Chevalier De Bretigny, sixteen of his officers, and two hundred of his enlisted men who were captured by the British Florida Navy. Included in this group was at least one person who would report back to France on the possibility of taking Saint Augustine. There were at least seventeen French vessels taken from the Charleston area with crews to Saint Augustine. These people were originally kept on Anastasia Island in the tower on the lighthouse. However as the group increased in size they were given liberty for the island. These men were finally sent on to the French Caribbean.

Dr. Father Pedro Camps was a Minorcan priest. Father Camps kept the records of the births, deaths, and marriages in the Minorcan community in a book today called the Golden Book of the Minorcans. November 9, 1777 in the New Smyrna church was transferred to Saint Augustine. Father Camps lived in Saint Augustine till his death in the 2nd Spanish period on May 19, 1790.

Reverend John Kennedy arrived in 1777 with a royal appointment to the Free Schools in East Florida as schoolmaster up to 1785. The subjects taught, according to a table of fees fixed by the Council in 1775, and included English, writing, arithmetic, Latin and Greek.

In May, 1777 American Colonel Samuel Elbert led an expeditionary force to invade Florida. His force totaled 600-800 men. He divided them into two groups, putting Colonel John Baker in charge of the land-based advance while he took the rest of the men aboard seven vessels to plow the coastal waters to the St. Mary River.

In 1763, the Spanish ceded Florida to the British in a trade for the port of Havana. The treaty was unclear as to the status of the Keys. An agent of the King of Spain claimed that the islands, rich in fish, turtles and mahogany for shipbuilding, were part of Cuba, fearing that the English might build fortresses and dominate the shipping lanes. The British also realized the treaty was ambiguous, but declared that the Keys should be occupied and defended as part of Florida. The British claim was never officially contested but no real government exercised control of the Keys. Most, if not all of the Florida indigenous natives had been killed or driven from their homeland by about 1763.

Key West and the entire chain of Keys provided many shipwrecks, lumbering, fishing and hiding areas, and fresh drinking water for every nation. The deep-water anchorage facility at Cayo Hueso (Key West) permitted anchoring for ships not wishing to stop in Havana or Charleston. It was a frequented by pirates, privateers and fisherman alike as well as those who made their living salvaging the shipwrecks caused by the treacherous coral reefs and tricky currents.

Age of Sail Glossary

aft: toward the stern (rear) of the ship.

ahead: in a forward direction

aloft: above the deck of the ship.

barque (bark): a three-masted vessel with the foremast and mainmast square-rigged and the mizzenmast fore-and-aft rigged.

belay: to make a rope fast to a belaying pin, cleat, or other such device. Also used as a general command to stop or cancel, e.g., "Belay that last order!"

belaying pin: a wooden pin, later made of metal, generally about twenty inches in length to which lines were made fast , or "belayed." They were arranged in pin rails along the inside of the bulwark and in fife rails around the masts.

binnacle: a large wooden box, just forward of the helm, housing the compass, half-hour glass for timing the watches, and candles to light the compass at night.

boatswain's chair: a wooden seat with a rope sling attached. Used for hoisting men aloft or over the side for work.

bosun: also boatswain, a crew member responsible for keeping the hull, rigging and sails in repair.

bow chaser: a cannon situated near the bow to fire as directly forward as possible.

bowsprit: a large piece of timber which stands out from the bow of a ship.

breeching: rope used to secure a cannon to the side of a ship and prevent it from recoiling too far.

brig: a two masted vessel, square rigged on both masts.

bulwarks: the sides of a ship above the upper deck.

bumboat: privately owned boat used to carry out to anchored vessels vegetables, liquor, and other items for sale.

burgoo: mixture of coarse oatmeal and water, porridge.

canister: musket ball size iron shot encased in a cylindrical metal cast. When fired from a cannon, the case breaks apart releasing the enclosed shot. (not unlike firing buckshot from a shotgun shell.)

Cat-O'-Nine Tails: a whip made from knotted ropes, used to punish crewmen. What was meant by being "flogged."

chase: a ship being pursued.

coxswain: (cox'n) The person in charge of the captain's personal boat.

cutter: a sailboat with one mast and a mainsail and two headsails.

dogwatch: the watches from four to six, and from six to eight, in the evening.

fathom: unit of measurement equal to six feet.

flotsam: Debris floating on the water surface.

forecastle: pronounced fo'c'sle. The forward part of the upper deck, forward of the foremast, in some vessels raised above the upper deck. Also, the space enclosed by this deck.

founder: used to described a ship that is having difficulty remaining afloat.

frigate: a fast three masted fully rigged ship carrying anywhere from twenty to forty-eight guns.

full and by: a nautical term meaning proceed under full sail.

furl: to lower a sail.

futtock shrouds: short, heavy pieces of standing rigging connected on one end to the topmast shrouds at the outer edge of the top and on the other to the lower shrouds, designed to bear the pressure on the topmast shrouds. Often used by sailors to go aloft.

gaff: a spar or pole extending diagonally upward from the after side of a mast and supporting a fore-and-aft sail.

galley: the kitchen area of a ship.

grapeshot: a cluster of round, iron shot, generally nine in all, and wrapped in canvas. Upon firing the grapeshot would spread out for a shotgun effect. Used against men and light hulls.

grating: hatch cover composed of perpendicular, interlocking wood pieces, much like a heavy wood screen. It allowed light and air below while still providing cover for the hatch. Gratings were covered with tarpaulins in rough or wet weather.

grog: British naval seaman received a portion of liquor every day. In 1740, Admiral Edward Vernon ordered the rum to be diluted with water. Vernon's nickname was Old Grogram, and the beverage was given the name grog in their disdain for Vernon.

gunwale: pronounced gun-el. The upper edge of a ship's side.

halyard: a line used to hoist a sail or spar. The tightness of the halyard can affect sail shape.

handsomely: slowly, gradually.

hard tack: ship's biscuit.

haul: pulling on a line.

heave to: arranging the sails in such a manner as to stop the forward motion of the ship.

heel: the tilt of a ship/boat to one side.

helm: the wheel of a ship or the tiller of a boat.

holystone: a block of sandstone used to scour the wooden decks of a ship.

idler: the name of those members of a ship's crew that did not stand night watch because of their work, example cook, carpenters.

jetty: a manmade structure projecting from the shore.

jib: a triangular sail attached to the headstay.

John Company: nickname for the Honourable East India Company

jolly boat: a small workboat.

jonathan: British nickname for an American.

keel: a flat surface (fin) built into the bottom of the ship to reduce the leeway caused by the wind pushing against the side of the ship.

ketch: a sailboat with two masts. The shorter mizzen mast is aft of the main, but forward of the rudder post.

knot: one knot equals one nautical mile per hour. This rate is equivalent to approximately 1.15 statute miles per hour.

larboard: the left side of a ship or boat.

lee: the direction toward which the wind is blowing. The direction sheltered from the wind.

leeward: pronounced loo-ard. downwind.

Letter of Marque: a commission issued by the governmental authorizing seizure of enemy property.

luff: the order to the steersman to put the helm towards the lee side of the ship, in order to sail nearer to the wind.

main mast: the tallest (possibly only) mast on a ship.

mast: any vertical pole on the ship that sails are attached to.

mizzen mast: a smaller aft mast.

moor: to attach a ship to a mooring, dock, post, anchor.

nautical mile: one minute of latitude, approximately 6076 feet – about 1/8 longer than the statute mile of 5280 feet.

pitch: (1) a fore and aft rocking motion of a boat. (2) a material used to seal cracks in wooden planks.

privateer: a privateer is a captain with a Letter of Marque which allows a captain to plunder any ship of a given enemy nation. A privateer was **supposed** to be above being tried for piracy.

prize: an enemy vessel captured at sea by a warship or privateer. Technically these ships belonged to the crown, but after review by the Admiralty court and condemnation, they were sold and the prize money shared.

powder monkey: young boy (usually) who carried cartridges of gunpowder from the filling room up to the guns during battle.

quadrant: instrument used to take the altitude of the sun or other celestial bodies in order to determine the latitude of a place. Forerunner to the modern sextant.

quarterdeck: a term applied to the afterpart of the upper deck. The area is generally reserved for officers.

quarter gallery: a small, enclosed balcony with windows located on either side of the great cabin aft and projecting out slightly from the side of the ship. Traditionally contained the head, or toilet, for use by those occupying the great cabin.

rake: a measurement of the top of the mast's tilt toward the bow or stern.

rate: Ships were rated from first to sixth rates based on their size and armament:

First rate	line of battle 100 or more guns on 3 gundecks
Second rate	line of battle 90 to 98 guns on 3 gundecks
Third rate	line of battle 80, 74 or 64 guns on 2 gundecks
Fourth rate	below the line 50 guns on 1 or 2 gundecks
Fifth rate	frigates 32 to 44 guns on 1 gundeck
Sixth rate	frigates 20 to 28 guns on 1 gundeck

ratline: pronounced ratlin. Small lines tied between the shrouds, horizontal to the deck, forming a sort of rope ladder on which the men can climb aloft.

reef: to reduce the area of sail. This helps prevent too much sail from being in use when the wind gets stronger (a storm or gale).

roll: a side-to-side motion of the ship, usually caused by waves.

schooner: a North American (colonial) vessel with two masts the same size.

scuppers: Drain holes on deck, in the toe rail, or in bulwarks.

scuttle: any small, generally covered hatchway through a ship's deck.

sextant: a navigational instrument used to determine the vertical position of an object such as the sun, moon or stars.

shoal: shallow, not deep.

shrouds: heavy ropes leading from a masthead aft and down to support the mast when the wind is from abeam or farther aft.

skiff: a small boat.

sky lark: to frolic or play, especially up in the rigging.

spar: any lumber/pole used in rigging sails on a ship.

starboard: the right side of a ship or boat.

stern: the aft part of a boat or ship.

stern chasers: cannons directed aft to fire on a pursuing vessel.

tack: to turn a ship about from one tack to another, by bringing her head to the wind.

taffrail: the upper part of the ship's stern, usually ornament with carved work or bolding.

thwart: seat or bench in a boat on which the rowers sit.

topgallant: the mast above the topmast, also sometimes the yard and sail set on it.

transom: the stern cross-section/panel forming the after end of a ship's hull.

veer: a shifting of the wind direction.

waister: landsman or unskilled seaman who worked in the waist of the ship.

wear: to turn the vessel from one tack to another by turning the stern through the wind.

weigh: to raise, as in to weigh anchor.

windward: the side or direction from which the wind is blowing.

yard: a spar attached to the mast and used to hoist sails.

yard arm: the end of a yard.

yawl: a two-masted sailboat/fishing boat with the shorter mizzen mast placed aft of the rudder post. Similar to a ketch.

zephyr: a gentle breeze. The west wind.